NANCY DREW ANTHOLOGY

NANCY DREW ANTHOLOGY

A Collection of Writing & Art
Featuring Everybody's Favorite Female Sleuth

Edited by
Melanie Villines

SILVER BIRCH PRESS
LOS ANGELES, CALIFORNIA

The Nancy Drew Anthology
is dedicated to the first Carolyn Keene,
Mildred Wirt Benson
(1905-2002)

INTRODUCTION

MELANIE VILLINES

Each day our blog (silverbirchpress.wordpress.com) features writing based on a specific theme. In early 2016, our theme was "Me, in Fiction," where authors imagined themselves as fictional characters. On January 2, 2016, the blog featured a poem by Jennifer Finstrom titled "Nancy Drew's Guide to Life," which elicited comments from many readers who said that Nancy Drew had been a significant influence in their lives—especially their development as readers and writers. This response sparked the idea for this collection—we issued a call for submissions in early January 2016, and received submissions from many corners of the globe.

Since her 1930 appearance in *The Secret of the Old Clock*, amateur sleuth Nancy Drew has inspired generations of girls—including this one—with her moxie, intelligence, determination, but most of all independence. After nearly a century, Nancy Drew is as popular as ever—with avid fans around the world. We're celebrating this female icon and role model with the *Nancy Drew Anthology: A Collection of Writing & Art Featuring Everyone's Favorite Female Sleuth*.

We wish to thank Jennifer Finstrom by kicking off the *Nancy Drew Anthology* with her poem that inspired the collection.

TABLE OF CONTENTS

NANCY DREW ANTHOLOGY

THE FIRST CLUE

JENNIFER FINSTROM

Nancy Drew's Guide to Life

"Moxie and a good sense of balance are essential when crawling
on a roof."
—*Nancy Drew's Guide to Life* by Jennifer Worick

I inspect *Nancy Drew's Guide to Life*
with a magnifying glass, hoping to find
the smallest connection between us. But I
don't know Morse code or how to throw
my voice. I don't drive a fancy blue roadster.
Nonetheless, the advice that "lipstick is not
just for looking glamorous; it can be used
to signal for help on windows and other
surfaces" convinces me that we are kindred
spirits, as does the notion that "dressing
well will open any doors, even those
connected to a top-secret factory."

And while I suspect I lack physical courage
and don't know how resourceful I might be
when faced with kidnappers, jewel thieves,
or smugglers, I'll keep in mind that
"flowers sent by secret admirers might
be coated with poison" and the pragmatic,
"when confused, sit back and try to arrange
the facts into some kind of order." I like
to believe I'd have plenty of moxie if I
needed it, that I could crawl on any roof,
no matter how high or how metaphorical.

PASSWORD TO NANCY DREW

Nancy made a wild scramble

SUJOY BHATTACHARYA

Homage to Nancy Drew

Embodiment of courage—Nancy Drew.
Abundance of boldness, Nancy Drew.
Your intelligence unparalleled.
You are the brightest star in the galaxy of female icons!
In thousands of hearts, you have kindled the lamp of fearlessness.
You are a pride to womanhood across the globe.
Many departed souls extend their invisible hands to bless you!
If you were a living soul, you would have been adored as a deity.
You have attained immortality—the most cherished longing of human beings.

BILL CAPOSSERE

That Hair

Oh, that hair. That evocative, enticing, uniquely-her-own Titian hair. I had no idea, of course, who Titian was in third grade, but I didn't need to know. The color was clear enough on those book covers: Nancy Drew kneeling demurely on the ground, taking apart the Old Clock; Nancy hiding behind the Whispering Statue or crouching in the Old Attic. Nancy dangling the Broken Locket. Or best of all, Nancy at Shadow Ranch atop a rearing horse—barely a Titian strand out of place even as she is standing in the stirrups and pulling back on the reins while the powerful creature beneath her shies in panic at the ghost horse in the background.

Oh, that hair. That bright reddish-gold hair always remarked upon by page three or five or seven. That hair and that exotic word—Titian. A word not in my vocabulary, having as far as I recall never been used in Danny Dunn, The Hardy Boys, Tom Swift, or any of the other books I was zipping through at that age, finishing them too quickly for my parents to replace them and so turning to my sister's books as well: Cherry Ames, Trixie Belden, Nancy Drew. A word I had to look up to learn how to pronounce, one that in its sibilant alien-ness bespoke an entire world of yet-to-be-experienced encounters. Both that hair and that word flamed so brilliantly in my imagination that the various illustrators' attempts to capture it were nearly foredoomed to failure, Nancy's hair on the covers inevitably too dull *(The Secret of the Golden Pavilion),* too fake *(The Ghost of Blackwood Hall),* or too typically blonde *(The Clue of the Leaning Chimney).*

But *The Secret of Shadow Ranch?* Cover artist Rudy Nappi nailed it. In a book where "She brushed her titian hair until it gleamed"—not the only time that exact phrase is used in the book by the way—Nappi got it all just right. The sheer physicality of the image and the wanton sense of motion and wild adventure (perhaps no surprise for an artist who also illustrated pulp fiction like *She Tried to Be Good* and *Reefer Girl*) went hand in hand with the inherent siren call of that red-gold hair. That horse might as well have kicked me in the head. I was a goner. Nancy Drew—my very first crush.

I'll admit, it set a pattern. Ginger on *Gilligan's Island*. Mary Jane Watson from *Spiderman* (c'mon Peter Parker, sooo much hotter than Gwen Stacey). The Iannone twins—Tammy and Toni—who lived in the house behind me. Jean Grey of the *X-Men*. Daphne from *Scooby Doo*. Josie, lead vocalist for the *Pussycats*.

Sarah who moved away in eighth grade, my last sight of her that red hair framed in a backlit bedroom window, out of reach in so many ways. Medusa from Marvel's *Inhumans*.

And yes, I duly note what seems to be a preponderance of fictional characters versus actual living redheads. I blame the math. Only four percent of the U.S. population has red hair, after all; my opportunities for flesh-and-blood encounters were therefore severely limited. At least, that's the excuse I'm going with.

Molly Ringwald in *The Breakfast Club*. Sue on the second floor of my freshman dorm at Syracuse. Claire from *Six Feet Under*.

The list may seem indiscriminate, but I do draw *some* lines. I don't fall for everyone whose head is dressed in red. Marvel's Medusa, yes, but not Poison Ivy—Batman's venomous villainess. I loved Ginger; I didn't love Lucy. Josie, but definitely not the Little Mermaid. It's a preference, not a perversion. Though I might cop to the lesser charge of an "obsession."

A word my wife might use as well, based on the conversations that regularly occur when she periodically asks me what color she should dye her hair to hide the increasing grey.

"What do you think—should I do Midnight Black?"

"How about red?"

"What about Ebony Mocha?"

"How about red?"

"What do you think of Chestnut?"

"I don't know; what do you think of red?"

"Auburn?"

"Getting closer. What about, I don't know, a red?"

"You really want red? Really? You mean like a bright red?"

"Have you ever read Nancy Drew?"

LINDA CROSFIELD

Tolling Bell

Nancy is expected to sip tea,
to be polite to elders,
to be perplexed, if only briefly,
by screams that pierce
and chandeliers that swing.

Whatever she does
is sure to involve an adverb.
When you're a teenage detective
there is little that doesn't take its toll.

JENNIFER FINSTROM

Moxie and Melancholy

"Since solving *The Secret of the Old Clock*, she had longed for
another case. Here was her chance!" —*The Hidden Staircase*

We talk about Nancy Drew one night in my writing group, and
someone asks about melancholy. Is there sorrow as well the
smoothly solved case? I don't know, but I wonder, and when I
get home, I take out *The Hidden Staircase*, the second book of
the series, and look for hints of sadness in River Heights.
Though not apparent on the page, I wonder if Nancy's mother's
death (mentioned in chapter one) still haunts her. I wonder, too,
about Ned Nickerson—her handsome and athletic boyfriend—
since sorrow and romance go hand in hand, and am shocked to
find that he doesn't exist yet, won't appear on the scene until
The Clue in the Diary (volume number seven) when he saves
Nancy's car from the wind-borne embers of a house fire.

In *The Hidden Staircase*, Nancy goes on a date with Dirk
Jackson, red-haired tennis star, before joining her friend
Helen at the haunted house. When Nancy waves goodbye to
Dirk as he drives away, she must know that this will one day
end, and perhaps she doesn't even care. And although I
don't find melancholy in any of the expected places,
Nancy's cheerful demeanor seems to be hiding something
potentially immense, some sense of a world that is at times
empty and ominous despite its episodic repetition. I like to
think that Nancy wakes regularly from dreams where she is
looking for something she cannot find: she shakes off the
dream as she brushes her hair, steps into her moxie like
stepping into her best pumps, and goes out in search of answers. She looks for more and more mysteries until at last
they are all that define her.

ALICE-CATHERINE JENNINGS

Nancy in Finland

Nancy is a fetching girl
a blue-eyed daughter
a fair-haired girl
an only child
who lives inside
a brick home
with her father
in a red house
on a tree-paved street
in an unnamed state
an only daughter.

Luckless daughter
with no mother
no one to hinder
her endeavors
a motherless child
with a court-man father
a favored offspring
a golden lass
in a dark blue car
with no cover
a ring-rich child
she has no mother.

A girlish girl
her father's daughter
a braid-hair lass
in sun-back dresses
she hits shuttlecocks
with lightweight rackets.
A boyish sleuth
a teen detective
she has no job
just a mission
to help the helpless
with her senses.

JENNIFER HERNANDEZ

Nancy Drew is my kind of princess

    flashlight scepter in hand
Sleuthing through secret passages,
    tunnels, attics, caves
Girl detective slays her own dragons
    needs no rescue
Sheathed in smart frocks with
    matching handbags
Strawberry blonde hair
    tucked behind one ear
Clues deduced
    mysteries solved
Blue roadster
    speeding into the sunset

JENNIFER LAGIER

Sleuth
" . . . as cool as Mata Hari and as sweet as Betty Crocker . . ."
—Bobbie Ann Mason

Nancy Drew, you were exactly
what this naïve country girl needed.
Inquisitive and assertive,
you were a positive prototype
for generations of professional women.
Taught us to persevere,
dispassionately analyze,
constantly question.
Provided a model
of poise, independence.
I marveled at your cool skill
at unraveling mysteries,
identifying bad guys,
playing detective.
Mourned when you were cut down
to less-threatening size,
transformed from dominant force
into decorative female.

KATHLEEN A. LAWRENCE

Detecting Nancy Drew
(spiraling abecedarian)

           Anonymity
accurately belies
begetting clues.
  Capital D for detective,
     Drew emerges
 elegantly fashionable and
fearless, a gamely
  guiding heroine
 honoring inductive
inferences to judge
justly with knowledge,
kindness, and loyalty.
 Learning magnifies
meaning and nuance.
   Nancy   obscures
oddities, and problems
presenting questions.
Quizzically revealing to
  readers sanguine
 secrets. Tangled
   time,   unblemished
unraveling volumes
 valued.   Whimsical, and
  willful experiences
  extend   youthful
yarns and zippy
  zest.

CATFISH MCDARIS

Hero of America

Nancy Drew a fictional amateur sleuth
is a 16-year-old detective, often described
as a super girl, she is as immaculate and
self-possessed as a Miss America

She is as cool as Mata Hari and as sweet
as Betty Crocker, Nancy is attractive and
amazingly talented she studied psychology
is familiar with the power of suggestion

Nancy is a fine painter, speaks French, can
run motor boats, she is a skilled driver, the
prodigy is a sure shot, an excellent swimmer,
skillful oarsman, expert seamstress, gourmet
chef, a fine bridge player, brilliantly plays

Tennis and golf, rides like a cowboy, Nancy
dances like Ginger Rogers and can administer
first aid like the Mayo brothers, never lacks for
money, travels often to faraway locations

When the Nancy Drew books were first written
it was in the Great Depression, people needed
hope and heroes, some escape into fantasy, she
was someone to treasure, a lucky wishing star.

LEE PARPART

Nancy drew

Whenever things got slow around River Heights, or when there were personnel changes over at the Stratemeyer Syndicate that upset her or made her feel less invested in her own development as a character, Nancy coped by drawing.

Her most fertile period as an artist came in the gap between books 7 and 11. Mildred A. Wirt, aka the first Carolyn Keene, was on strike to protest the lowering of freelance rates at the syndicate during the Depression, and had been replaced by a male journalist, who wrote books 8, 9, and 10.

To distract herself from the loss of her preferred author, Nancy drew. In the couple of years that passed between *The Clue in the Diary* and *The Clue of the Broken Locket*, she completed at least a dozen self-portraits, crowding most of them onto a single large sheet of paper left behind by one of the Stratemeyer illustrators. For each drawing or set of drawings, she used a different method to capture some aspect of her appearance or some element of her character that she suspected might have been missed.

The first two sessions took the form of a mystic, Dada-style experiment in automatic writing, with Nancy wearing a blindfold and giving herself exactly one minute per portrait. Instead of drawing her own features, she sketched a rough outline of her body, then attempted, without being able to look at the lines, to fill the image with written notes.

The first one made her look like a polar bear and overflowed with adjectives handed down by various members of the team responsible for her creation: Peppy, Plucky, Curious, Kind.

The other attempt, which came out looking more like a real female silhouette, contained words and phrases not heard around the office, but whose meanings resonated with her as possible clues to her overpowering, lifelong need to identify and solve mysteries. Unflinching. Dogged. Determined. And a more shadowy phrase that was just coming into parlance in America at the time: anti-authoritarian.

In a bad experiment never to be repeated, Nancy drew one portrait of herself *while driving* her blue roadster through the center of River Heights. This was deeply out of character and almost had dire consequences when Nancy hopped a curb near the soda shop and came close to hitting a young couple in mid-kiss.

An equally frivolous, though much less risky, formal approach involved using vegetable-based watercolors to create a simple portrait of herself driving the roadster, then using treats to encourage Togo to lick the image until it took on a loose, indistinct quality that made her think of beaches and Toulouse-Lautrec.

In homage to both M.C. Escher and her main creator, Nancy once depicted herself as half a silhouette in the process of being drawn by the curved hand of Mildred Wirt. Nancy knew Mildred was a writer, not an artist, but she wanted to be sure to give the almost forgotten original author due credit for her own existence.

In one final drawing carried out shortly before Mildred was reinstated, Nancy used a magnifying glass to closely inspect the skin of her forearm, and devoted herself to reproducing exactly what she saw there. Good detecting was about learning how to look, and she wanted to test her skills at observation with an abstract visual puzzle. She focused intently on this task for several days, finally producing an intricately detailed, almost *trompe-l'oeil*, rendering of a one-inch patch of skin that included a network of criss-crossing lines not visible to the naked eye, punctuated by a small brown birthmark that she had known was there, but never bothered to explore. At the end of this intense period of struggle and reflection, she felt she knew herself better than at any other point in her story.

Nancy drew until she became tired of drawing. Mildred Wirt returned to the publishing house later that week, almost as though she was summoned back by the creative energies of her own creation. With Stratemeyer's personnel problems solved, Nancy sat down next to her author and began to think about writing.

DAVID PERLMUTTER

Word to the Mother: A Prose Poem

I thought I heard you say it was a pity that Nancy Drew never had any children.

But you're wrong. You're so wrong.

Nancy has thousands of them. Thousands of them.

All girls. Some women, actually.

And all fictional, like her. But that's beside the point.

Nancy is where it all begins for the independent-minded, risk-taking, gutsy American lady who has dominated the country's popular culture for almost a century.

Before her, there were few young women with her characteristics that weren't presented as evil villains. To be tamed, and thus ignored.

But you could not ignore a girl who could solve a mystery using only her brain and her intuition, with not a gun or any other kind of weapon for protection in sight. A girl who, when wanting to do right by somebody, never stopped until she did it. A girl who didn't let anyone—even her lawyer father, from whom she clearly inherited her great intelligence—stop her.

Nor did she let physical obstacles stop her. If she had to jump over a hedge or swim across a river in pursuit of a clue or a culprit, she did it. No questions asked.

And let it not be forgotten that it took two Hardy Boys to do the job of one Nancy Drew.

And other than perhaps those guys, and her spiritual older brother, Ellery Queen, not that many detectives with such a consistent, adaptable presence in American popular culture.

Her legacy is everywhere if you look close enough.

Think about the platoon of intrepid female P.I.s that rule the roost in mystery fiction today. Sharon McCone and Kinsey Millhone and V.I. Warshawski all clearly read and appreciated Nancy as kids. Otherwise, would they have pursued her line of work on a professional basis, and have been every bit as good as her doing it?

Same goes for all the tough-as-nails lady cops in every country's media. Do you really think all the paint-by-numbers police programs on the tube now would exist without them? And none would exist without Nancy.

And she's an even bigger influence in things directly targeted at her own original demographics, kids and teenagers. Lisa Simpson is her kissing cousin, able to get justice and speak her mind in a way Nancy herself would admire. The Powerpuff Girls put her philosophy into action all the time (Blossom more than the others). Would Kim Possible have been able to brag about her ability to do "anything" if Nancy hadn't done it all first? Would Candace Flynn expend so much energy and time trying to "bust" her brothers if Nancy hadn't been "busting" people before Candace was conceived? And speaking of Disney, what about the hit movie *Zootopia?* Isn't the female lead, Judy Hopps, Nancy as a cop in lagomorphian form?

The answer is "yes." They all are Nancy, and she is all of them.

There were other influences on the gutsy modern American girl, I know. Like Wonder Woman. But it often seems to me that in those cases the creators just put Nancy's brain into a super-powered body for backup. Same with every heroine with "Girl" or "Woman" at the end of her name, or not. Especially the ones that are around now, who can spit fire and kick ass even better than the men can sometimes.

Nancy is the one. The one they all know and love. And her example led them all to greatness.

She is the Mother. She is, sisters, the great spirit that made you all.

JEANNIE E. ROBERTS

Nancy Drew, the Everywoman

Evolving over six decades, and,
at times, exhibiting contradictory
values and a paradoxical nature,

her character did demonstrate two
things consistently: the inclusion
of flashlight and a connection

with readers. Feminists saluted
her female empowerment while
conservatives nodded to her middle-

class ways. Nancy was a role model
of strength and perseverance,
the good-deed doer, and the essence

of the term *everyman*. An *everywoman*
icon, Nancy was an everyday woman
who had just about everything,

including an everlasting appeal with
women readers nearly everywhere
in the world.

HILARY A. SMITH

The Enduring Appeal of Nancy Drew

Why do we love Nancy Drew and why has she continued to fascinate us for almost ninety years? The most obvious answer is, of course, that Nancy embodies many of the qualities any society should wish for its young women—and young men, for that matter—and that those young women might wish for themselves.

First, Nancy is, above all, curious and eager to attain knowledge. While many girls of her generation might recoil at the thought (let alone sight) of the snakes in the tapestry in the zigzag house in *The Crooked Banister*, Nancy is interested and asks Ned many questions about snake species and lore. Examining the tapestry, she queries, "What's this beautiful snake called—the one the fiery serpent is devouring?" (70). Her bright and eager mind files away this knowledge should it be useful later on.

This acquisition of knowledge often helps Nancy in times of need. Nancy's knowledge of automobiles, how to escape from a locked cellar or tack room, how to loosen ropes, and how to administer first aid all play a role in her many cases. In the 1931 version of *The Secret at Shadow Ranch* she is an excellent markswoman, shooting a lynx to save the lives of Bess and George. And although in *The Secret in the Old Attic*, "Ned took complete charge of the situation" (166) in freeing Nancy from the ropes Riggin Trott has used to bind her, she hardly sits around waiting to be rescued. She thinks, "I must get out of here!" and begins considering ways to attract attention so would-be rescuers can find her.

Nancy's independence in an era when young women were encouraged to see dating and, eventually, marriage as the pinnacle of feminine achievement, is both inspiring and encouraging. In *The Crooked Banister,* Nancy is described as dating Ned "almost exclusively" (59); clearly she is too wise to tie herself down prematurely, as many other young women of her generation might have. While Ned, Dave, and Burt often join and assist Nancy, George, and Bess while working on cases, Nancy never neglects her girls in favor of boys. The girl-centric bent to the Nancy Drew Mystery Stories is refreshing. Boys may assist us, but we are the stars of our own stories.

While Nancy is clever and sassy and stands up for herself, she never loses her manners or grace. She level-headedly defends herself when Mrs. Aldrin scoffs, "She's only a girl!" at the thought of a teenaged detective (55). "'I think,' Nancy answer[s], 'that you should consult my father. He's a lawyer. As you said, I'm only a teenage detective'" (57). Nancy's dead mother would be proud of the young lady her daughter has become.

As a girl reader, I envied fictional preteen and teenaged girls with occupations that transcended the role of babysitter. They weren't just entrepreneurs with a clever and independent means of earning money after school. Rather, they defined themselves through their occupations. Nancy never made the world of work seem mundane; instead, she imbued it with freedom and glamour, hopping into her blue roadster (later convertible) to investigate a crime, meet a client, or attend an event at Emerson College.

One of the most fascinating aspects of Nancy Drew is that she is a father-raised feminist. The father-daughter relationship that the Drews enjoy is characterized by trust and confidence but within safe parameters. For example, in *The Crooked Banister,* Bess and George must join Nancy in Mountainville if she is to stay on after Mr. Drew's return home to River Heights. Mr. Drew has raised her to be strong and confident. As he tells the client, "Mrs. Melody, I always give Nancy hard assignments and always with great confidence that she will come up with the right answers" (27). There is no infantilization or cloying daddy's girl, baby girl, or princess treatment in Carson Drew's relationship with his daughter. Perhaps the fact that Mr. Drew raises Nancy without the assistance of Nancy's mother has freed Nancy from some of the limiting stereotypes of her era. We wonder if Mrs. Drew were alive would she view Nancy's ambitions as a sleuth to be forward and unfeminine. Of course Carson Drew is helped by housekeeper Hannah Greun, but the primary influence in Nancy's life is her father.

Like many great characters in fiction, Nancy is an orphan. Admittedly, she is a half-orphan but with the absence of her mother, Nancy, like all great literary orphans before her, has the opportunity to create herself almost from scratch. Another fictional girl sleuth, eleven-year-old chemist Flavia de Luce from Alan Bradley's series, is also half-orphaned, having lost her mother in a mountaineering accident in Tibet. Perhaps for both Nancy and Flavia, the loss of the mother figure creates not just the opportunity for self-invention, but also the need for a search for self.

Nancy Drew and the Mystery of the Endless Clue

1.

You suspect clues led somewhere
and if they end up as a dead end,
disappointment
is just another mystery to explore,

a red herring,
and I do not like the taste or smell of herring

but I do like it
when a bad guy
gets his just desserts.

2.

A magnifying glass can bring things
up close and personal, make
the unknown clearer, and
the small details no longer seem
insignificant.

A microscope finds this amazing.

3.

Sometimes,
I think the bad guys want to be caught
so they leave evidence
all over the place
like bread crumbs
left by Hansel and Gretel

maybe
they are making it easy to find them

thinking I must be an empty-headed girl
with nothing on my mind
except boys
and matching my outfit

they do not know whom they are dealing with

I am a force to be reckoned with
a force like gravity
with common sense

clues are for boys
like the Hardy Boys
who cannot find their way
out of the first chapter
if you gave them a map
with a large X on it

4.

Sometimes
I believe I am real
and then
the overwhelming conclusions
tell me otherwise

5.

On a clear day, light is suspicious
and clouds are daggers from a villain's eyes

6.

suspect everyone
trust no one
not your friends
or family
or yourself ➤

anyone
everyone
is capable of mischief

7.

When it rains,
clues splash me with resolutions.

Melancholy wears a yellow raincoat.

My best friend is my own cloudy disposition
that allows me to be firm, yet fair,
with a keen eye for danger in every situation.

Without certain aloofness,
I would be in trouble all the time
instead of ahead of everyone else,
even my own shadow,

and who likes a damsel in distress?

I know some men
would prefer I swoon at a mouse
or show a molecule of fear,

but I am confident,
and that
mystifies them.

PARTNERS IN CRIME

KATHLEEN M. HEIDEMAN

Nancy pulled

KATHLEEN HOGAN

Saving Ned Nickerson

Where was Ned? He was very late, too tardy to be hardy,
out of character for one so steady, ready to lend a hand.

Dinner grew cold, so late it might grow mold, as Nancy
waited, agitated, sure to her classic pump soles something was amiss.

It was intolerable, unacceptable, money was gone, and with so many
in need. Was it in the clock, under a rock, beneath a staircase, down a well?

The foliage overgrown with time and the god-awful heat
blocked vision, until all coherence fled, yet she persisted,

her downy downed blond hair hung in locks, mighty fair,
tailored white shirt and navy skirt, only slightly soiled, tattered.

But with bruised lips, color smeared, raccoon blue eyes,
she still hurled and hummed, blazed, knighted.

Nancy Drew knew the scoop, had the answers
read the clues, she drove pell-mell, whatever that meant,

in her roadster forward; Ned's only hope, his rescuer, savior.
The evil would be thwarted, conclusion achieved, nasty plotters jailed.

Oh, so simple this world! Good vs. evil; the tension, tight, taut, strained.
Youth stood tall, a firewall; brave, strong, determined, justified.

And we took solace from Nancy, knew she wouldn't resist the lure,
a thread dangling irresistible, the quest all important, needing to know . . .

. . . Who did it!!?!

JULEIGH HOWARD-HOBSON

Unwrapping the 11th Nancy Drew Book at My Birthday Party, 1972

The cover of *The Clue Of The Broken*
Locket shows all three girls, Nancy, Bess and
George. Nancy's in the middle, the token
Clue (a heart locket) dangling from her hand.
There's a rowboat. All three girls are holding
Their shoes, no, their sneakers, which match their shirts:
Pink for George, yellow for Nancy (Golden
Girl that she is), blue for Bess. They're experts
At solving mysteries. The cover is
Perfectly wrought—danger looms from tree
Branches and in the reeds. Whatever is
Going on is going on at dusk. See
How the sky is pink and blue? It's an ache,
The itch to read it, but first: ice cream. . . . cake . . .

Ode to the Nancy Drew Books

I read enough of them to figure out
there was a formula: time and again,
blonde Nancy tracks the villains to their den,
then slips and ends up flailing like a trout
in her foes' deadly net. Those dastards hiss
menacing lines in dialect, then tie
up fragile Nancy, leaving her to die . . .
Perhaps the authors were rope fetishists.

Of Nancy's gal pals, I most liked George Fayne,
androgynously named tomboyish teen
who, like me, had a close-cropped jet-black mane.
I whooped with joy, pretending not to see
the text describing George's eyes as green:
    At last!! A character who looks like me!

KRISTIE BETTS LETTER

Which Nancy Drew Girl Are You?

1. If you have a passion for detail, you are NANCY
in the forefront, in the sweater set, sharp but kind, always sporting something cute, saving the boys, the men, the old ladies, but taking the girls with you—notice the clues in the old clocks, the new docks, the mismatched socks, and notice the contradictions between eyes and mouths, the sounds that weren't the wind, were never just the wind, the devil is in those details.

2. If you have a passion for people, you are BESS
the pleasantly plump but still pretty, the nervous but braver-with-friends, the swinging hair and heaving bosom type, sweet as marmalade, replete with mama, ready for adventure but not until necessary, for conversations, for exultations, for excitations, and for the yummy treats, laid out on trays, by men who never turn their eyes away, hungry.

3. If you have passion, just plain old passion, you are GEORGE
the one with secrets, the currents running beneath, the buzz and spark of new energy, wind on the nape, made possible by hair kept short, the laughter too loud, the fascination with the shape of Nancy's mouth when she spoke, to let her hand linger on arm too long, to feel each individual strawberry blonde hair—don't let Buck or Burt fool you, no fear here.

Reading Aloud

Nancy Drew solves many a
mystery in my daughter's voice
while I do the dishes. My mind
floats like soap suds. She
becomes Nancy. I worry about
not being in the brick house
waiting for the blue roadster to
pull in. Nancy's mother is dead.
The girl sleuth gets into sticky
situations, but her friends rescue
her. It's usually the girl named
George who thinks fast, not the
one named Bess who is plump
like my little reader. Ned seems
like a solid kind of boyfriend,
but I don't know enough about
him.

ROBERT PERRET

Nancy Drew and the Secret of the Gravedigger

"Hold the lantern steady, Bess!" The chill of the damp grass beneath her knees was sending shivers throughout Nancy's body. It was the last thing she wanted as she tried to spin the tiny wheels on the widow's decoder ring.

"I don't think we should be out here by ourselves!" Bess had hunched down into her pink woolen coat so that her eyes just peeped out above her collar. Every time she heard a noise in the cemetery she jumped, and every time she jumped Nancy lost her light.

"Relax, would you?" George said. "No one knows we're here. How could they?" Her manner seemed cavalier but her knuckles were white, wrapped around the shovel handle. "Just hurry it up, Nancy. This lantern is blotting out our night vision."

"Got it!" Nancy waved her notebook in triumph. "We were right, this strange old headstone is a secret message. It will lead us right to the to the catacomb!"

"And right to Helen!" George said.

"I hope she's all right. I'd die of fright in a spooky old place like this," Bess said.

"Don't worry, Bess," Nancy said. "Helen is only in this mess because of her brave heart, and that will see a girl through anything."

"I can't believe she climbed right up into the widow's dusty attic all by herself, just to get a look at some old luggage."

"They were footlockers lugged home from Gettysburg. The original deed to the old manor is in there. It will prove the Talbots are frauds and that Mrs. Shelby is the rightful heir."

"I know it's important, Nancy, but is it important enough for Helen to risk her life?"

"The truth is always that important!"

"Besides," George chimed in, "there's nothing up in that attic but dust bunnies and cobwebs."

50

"Helen didn't know that for certain. She's in a frightful mess now, isn't she?"

"Of course she isn't!"

"Kidnapped by the Gravedigger, buried alive here in this creepy old place, and on the eve of the big dance to boot! If that isn't trouble I don't know what is."

"You're forgetting one thing, Bess," George took her by the shoulders. "Helen is a personal friend of the three best detectives in River Heights, and we won't let anything stop us!"

"All right, girls, enough foolishness." Nancy plucked her trusty compass from her pocket and pressed her heels against the tombstone. "Ten steps north . . ." Nancy swung her legs forward in giant strides.

"Why are you walking like that, Nancy?"

"This nursery rhyme wasn't made with girl detectives in mind. In fact, I fancy whoever made this puzzle didn't count on us at all. If we want to follow in the steps of this criminal we're going to have to walk like a man. Hike up your hems, ladies!"

And so the trio tromped through the dark cemetery, tamping the lantern and relying on the moon to show the way. Nancy charged forth brandishing her notebook, Bess hugged herself inside her coat, and George wielded the shovel like a Roman spear bearer. They heard only the crunching of their feet and the gasping of their breath. Nancy was leading them to the far end of the cemetery. As they passed, the headstones became worn and pitted, shrinking in size and eventually becoming not much more than rocks crudely inscribed with names. According to the few dates they could read, they had traveled back generations from the fresh graves of the 1930s to stand on the interred remains of Civil War soldiers.

"Just think, our great, great, great grandfathers could be right here," Bess remarked.

"I only care about getting Helen out of here. The rest of these fellows can rest in peace as far as I am concerned," George replied.

51

"This is where the trail ends," Nancy said, resting against a gnarled tree stump. "Spread out and see what you can find. Look for footprints, fresh signs of digging, anything."

George thrashed the underbrush with her shovel, like Alan Quartermain looking for a lost city in some primordial jungle. Bess tiptoed around, running her fingertips across the monuments and whispering the names to herself. Nancy was on the ground, probing with fingers and eyes for the prints of the Gravedigger's great boots. She'd committed the shape to memory when the girls had come pounding on the door of the old manor, demanding that the Widow Talbot release Helen. That horrible old lady had only cackled and shut the door, but Nancy had seen the mud tracked in and out the front door across the wooden porch. Normally, Mrs. Talbot would never have allowed that kind of thing. More importantly, the prints were deeper exiting the house, heavier. Mrs. Talbot had summoned the Gravedigger from his shack, allowed him to leave a mess of graveyard mud across her carpets, all so he could drag poor Helen away. They'd followed his tracks to where he'd entered his truck, and followed those tire ruts to the cemetery. He'd parked on the road, the graves too thick to drive through, but he knew this land, his home. Somehow, he'd picked his way across without leaving a sign.

Helen was sure her friends wouldn't be far behind. She'd left the ring lying in the bed of the man's truck. Whether he hadn't realized its significance, or if he was just too shy to frisk a girl, she'd managed it. Smuggled out the ring and left it for them, a beacon. Nancy had seen the strange symbols on the ring before—they all had. As kids they had dared each other to touch the Witch's Stone, a large tombstone with cryptic writing. It was believed all of the witches in old River Heights had been buried there, in one mass grave in the seventeenth century—their coven returned to their dark master. Nancy knew that was nonsense. George secretly hoped it was true. Bess just didn't want to think about what it might represent. She'd never touched the Witch's Stone as a child, had never even seen it until tonight. Once, Nancy had spent the night in front of it. That had been enough to prove her mastery over the superstition. George had puzzled over it, often traipsing out here in the middle of the night, hoping for some wondrous, horrible thing to happen. They had all known where that ring pointed. After solving its riddle and following its instructions, they were left to ponder in a seemingly empty field.

"We could be digging all night and not find her," George said.

"There has to be freshly turned earth somewhere," Nancy insisted. "They didn't just disappear."

"Will you two stop saying such ghastly things!" Bess turned up the lantern again.

"Turn it back down. Do you want the Gravedigger to know where we are?" George told her.

"If he doesn't know by now he's a fool, and no fool could fool Nancy like this," Bess responded.

"Bess is right, we might as well give the lantern a chance."

Bess puffed up with satisfaction and plunked the lantern on the huge stump with a resounding clank.

"What was that noise?" George wondered.

"There's something strange about that stump," Nancy said.

She moved the lantern to the ground and put her ear to the stump before rapping smartly upon it.

"Hollow," she declared.

The three began poking and prodding it, scrutinizing every inch. Nancy felt the wood give beneath her fingers with a sigh. She'd found a latch! The stump opened to reveal a door set into the earth like a storm cellar. It was closed with a tumbler lock. Scratched into the door were three of the strange symbols. Nancy quickly decoded them with the ring. The lock opened smoothly, but it took all three girls working together to pull the massive door aside.

In the musty darkness below they heard a frantic scuffle. Nancy thrust down the lantern and they saw Helen bound in ropes, thrashing over the shoulder of the Gravedigger—a lumbering brute, forced to crouch low in the confined space of the catacomb. In a moment, George leapt past Nancy and brought down the shovel upon the Gravedigger's back. He yowled with pain and dropped Helen before retreating to the far corner. Nancy slipped in and lifted Helen to a seated position before slipping off the rag binding her mouth. George pressed her advantage and the Gravedigger cowered.

"Stop!" Bess cried from the world above. "Can't you see that he's frightened?"

"How do you think he made Helen feel?" George said, taking a swing at the man, who, to everyone's surprise, seemed to disappear.

Nancy held the lantern towards the far corner where the Gravedigger had been, revealing a large gap. Nancy moved against the wall and put the lantern through at arm's length.

"Be careful, he might grab you!" Bess warned.

"He is long gone," Nancy replied. "This crack opens up into a cavern filled with alcoves for the dead. When they named this place the catacombs, they weren't kidding. There are tunnels beyond. Where they come out, who knows? Besides the Gravedigger, I mean."

After George released the ropes binding her, Helen stretched out the kinks in her muscles.

"It was awfully swell of you girls to come rescue me."

"It was awfully foolish of you to go up into that attic, Helen!" Bess chided. "You gave us an dreadful fright!"

"What happened up there anyway?"

"I waited until old Widow Talbot had gone to bed, I could tell by the light going dark in her window. I slipped in the kitchen door and made my way up the stairs. They creaked once or twice, but I guess to an old woman in an old house that's nothing. I stood on a chair to pull down the attic ladder. That kicked up a fearsome cloud of dust, and I had to stifle an attack of sneezes. I thought the caper was up then for sure, but after I waited a minute and heard nothing I climbed on up. There's a proper museum up there, with old guns, sewing machines, dresses, and hats. I just about jumped out of my skin when my

54

little candle revealed a person hiding in the dark. Turns out it was just a painting of Mr. Talbot, back in his heyday. Just as I breathed a sigh of relief, the trapdoor slammed shut behind me. I ran back and pounded on it but the door was shut tight. Below I heard Mrs. Talbot and her horrible laugh."

"Just you wait, my pretty," she said. "Little Joseph knows how to handle a sneak thief like you."

"I knew that I was trapped but good, but I also knew we'd never get another chance at that deed."

"That's a brave girl!" George crowed.

"Don't encourage her!" Bess whispered.

"Quickly, I ransacked the chests. Some were women's clothes, some too new, two were empty, and those I quickly passed over. Finally, in the back corner I found it, a moldering military trunk. Inside were a couple of old uniforms, rusty sabers, a few knick-knacks, and a bundle of papers. Flipping through, it was mostly personal correspondence, a few receipts, a photograph of a group of soldiers. Just as I heard voices below, I found a letter where Corporal Talbot described how he'd filched the manor deed right out of the dying hands of a Captain Shelby. The deed was enclosed, the letter said, but there was no deed or even an envelope for it to be enclosed in."

"Drat! All this danger for nothing!" Bess said.

"The trap door was flung open, and I could see a great silhouette looming toward me. I flung the bundle of paper at it, and pressed myself as far back into the dark as I could. Little Joseph, the Gravedigger, was upon me. He dragged me out to his truck and tied me up."

"We know the rest," Nancy said. "Bess is right, a lot of bother and Mrs. Talbot has her evil way in the end."

"A girl learns a thing or two being the friend of Nancy Drew," Helen smiled, before pulling an old piece of paper from her blouse.

"The deed! Mrs. Shelby and the manor are saved!"

DONNA JT SMITH

The Missing Mother's Message

I am forever near,
Oh, daughter dear, with titian hair;
I want to hold you, dry that tear
From your cheek so young and fair.

Oh, daughter dear, with titian hair,
My wish, just a whisper away
From your cheek so young and fair,
Is that you'll flourish day by day.

My wish, just a whisper away,
Though I'm not there to lean upon,
Is that you'll flourish day by day;
With fiery courage, grow up strong.

Though I'm not there to lean upon,
No loving mother-daughter talk,
With fiery courage, grow up strong,
Just mind the daily path you walk.

No loving mother-daughter talk
To keep you safe from harm;
Just mind the daily path you walk,
Hold fast my diary and charm.

To keep you safe from harm,
I want to hold you; dry that tear,
Hold fast my diary and charm,
I am forever near.

MYSTERIOUS INFLUENCE
(Nancy & Me)

AMANDA ARKEBAUER

Nancy Drew Quilt

KATHLEEN AGUERO

Larkspur Lane

A grey-haired woman in a wheelchair is locked up
on the grounds of a mansion against her will,
guarded by an imposter nurse until she's signed over her property
to the crooked lawyer running towards her, arm raised, face contorted,
shouting, *Get away from that fence!*
The elderly woman, finger to lips, catches Nancy's eye and points at him
as if our younger selves could free our older selves through stealth.
When I was Nancy's age, I couldn't imagine my efficient mother
in a nursing home, looking for a way out, whispering
that I should leave while I could or telling me I'd burn in hell
for what I'd done to her. She was clever.
She found the wooden gate where they put the garbage out.
She pulled, but it was locked. She waited, but no one came,
so she joined the other walkers, round and round the halls,
out one door, in the other, shuffling in untied shoes or stepping briskly,
imaginary briefcases or shopping bags under their arms as they made their way
through crowded streets from the train station to the office. They tried
all the passwords: *Call me a cab. I have to pick up the kids.*
Is it time to leave for the ballgame yet? One man nearly broke out,
but, ever polite, he paused to let me pass and the nurse came running,
pulling him back, scolding, *Get away from the door.*
Don't worry, the receptionist told me. *If they get as far as the lobby,*
an alarm rings. To sneak in and out of Larkspur Lane, you'd have to be
a sleuth, but now I've got the password. My mother
gave it to me. Lean close. I'll tell you what it is.

KIMMY ALAN

Dear Nancy Drew,

Do you have a clue as to how many boys, like me, have fallen in love with you? How can such a sleuth for the truth, be so oblivious to the legion of adolescent male admirers who dream of looking into your eyes of blue?

Intelligent, independent, and pretty, you're the template of what I and other boys thought a girlfriend ought to be. Your novels inspired within me countless puppy love fantasies of you and me, solving mysteries. How I wish, Nancy Drew, that you'd dream the same daydreams as I do.

Just imagine, how you and I would make the perfect crime-fighting duo. Together we'll uncover the secret identities of the cult members of The Black Snake Colony. We'll rescue heiress Laura Pendleton from her evil guardian. Together we'll ride Shadow Ranch at midnight where we'll chase the phantom horse out of sight. Afterwards, we'll hold hands and spark, and you'll declare me your beau, and I'll call you my sweetheart.

But, alas, like so many other fellas, my love will go unrequited. So pretty Nancy Drew, private gumshoe, if you happen to read this, take a cue. And discover how many boys, like me, are madly in love with you.

Oh, Nancy Drew, how I want to kiss you!

Love,
Kimmy Alan

ROBERTA BEARY

valentine's day

valentine's
day —

long hours in bed

with nancy drew

ANNE BORN

It's Not the Books, It's the Library

It's easy to identify the Nancy Drew and Dana Girls mysteries as my favorite children's adventure stories. When I read those little books, I wanted to be the one with the answer, the one to solve the crime, the one to show the grownups that this teen could do it. These girls were resourceful and clever. What's interesting to me now is that, for the life of me, I cannot recall a single episode, and I couldn't name more than one title. I do not remember just exactly what these plucky heroines accomplished. What I do remember is my cousin Diane.

Diane was much older than me. She was a child of the 1940s whose father served in WWII. She spent countless hours with my grandparents and her aunt and uncle, laying a foundation of trust and love for all of the cousins to follow. We all knew that we were important, and we knew that our family had something special—and a good bit of that came from the first cousin on the scene: Diane.

I came to know Nancy Drew because Diane collected the books. As far as I can remember, it was a complete set. I could borrow them, read them one at a time or a couple at a go, and return them to her collection. But it was never about the plot of the books, it was that Diane could read and when she did, she did it up in style. I could take books out of the town public library certainly, and I did that nearly every week I was in school. But Diane *had* a library and that was exciting to me.

Because my family did not have a budget line for book buying or the means to get to bookstores very often, and because I spent so much time at the library, I have only a dozen or so books from my childhood. I do not have all the great pirate books that I loved. I don't have the stories of Pompeii that I remember so clearly. And I don't have the Nancy Drew books. I vowed that when I had my own children, I would buy them books instead of just taking them to the library. I wanted them to know what Diane must have known, that there is tremendous comfort in being in a library, but there is something so much more powerful in owning a library.

Diane left us a few years ago. She had a heart ailment that would take her from us way too soon. In writing this, I am sad she doesn't know the lifelong impact her choice in teen fiction had on me. I want her to know that her collecting Nancy Drew and Dana Girl mysteries, and sharing them the way she did, instilled in me a love of libraries as well as a love of a great mystery story. My library has books about everything!

I'm reading my own copy of *The Daughter of Time* by Josephine Tey now with my book club and even though it does not feature a boyfriend with a slick convertible or helpful aunts and uncles, it does remind me of the debt I owe to my cousin Diane. It's great to have a library card, but it's even better to have a library.

TANYA BRYAN

Library Copy of The Password to Larkspur Lane

A mystery before the mystery begins!
Who wrote these words
Written in the margins
In English and Japanese?

First three pages scribbled with
Chirography only the author
(not Carolyn Keene)
Would understand
Left for library patrons thereafter
To try to decipher
The meaning
Of rewritten sentences:
"broadly—He always have that broadly smile"
"waxed—She wrapped the bouquet with waxed paper to prevent the germs"
"moan—Hannah moaned when she saw the plane crashing into the curb"

None of the translations
Quite match the original
But the clues are clear:
Nancy Drew appeals to everyone.

ASHINI J. DESAI

Discovering the Mysterious Mannequin

It was the summer of 1978, I was about ten years old, and the soundtrack to *Grease* was everywhere. We spent the summer days outside with our neighborhood friends in Queens, New York. We rode our bikes around the neighborhood or walked to the library with armloads of books. It was that summer when our elderly neighbor Charlotte invited my family for dinner. I remember the formality of the invitation since it seemed odd since it was just next door and we saw her every day. It was a casual dinner with burgers in the backyard. As we were leaving, Charlotte gave me a few Nancy Drew books (1, 2, 3, and 47) as a gift. She didn't know if I had already read them, but thought I'd like to have them.

To be honest, I am not a fan of mysteries and never bothered with Nancy Drew or Hardy Boys books or shows. However, since Charlotte gave me the books so warmly, I felt a sense of obligation to read them. Above all, as an active library patron, I was thrilled to receive my own books, ones that I could keep forever. This was an absolute treat! In fact, it truly is *forever*, since I still have three of the four books.

I read the books in order, learning about the secrets of the old clock and hidden staircases. My impression of Nancy Drew was a confident and grown-up young woman, complete with a purse and perfectly smooth pencil skirts. She had her own car, and could drive to all of these adventures with George and Bess. Her boyfriend Ned was easygoing and vanilla, much like Ken and Barbie. Carson Drew must have known Atticus Finch as supportive single-father lawyers, while Hannah Gruen must have traded secrets with Alice from *The Brady Bunch* as efficient housekeepers do. This is the stuff of fantasies and dreams. These quests happen to people on TV and in movies and books. Nancy's realm of River Heights was right there with Sandy,

Danny, and Rydell High. These are exotic worlds I wouldn't know in real life.

Book 47, *The Mysterious Mannequin*, was a game changer. Carolyn Keene brought Nancy's world close enough to touch the perimeter of mine. If this were a Venn diagram with a circle representing Nancy's domain and another circle for mine, as an Indian-American girl, this is where our circles overlapped slightly. True, the characters in this book were Turkish immigrants while we were Indian immigrants. However, that was enough for me.

The book cover art has a veiled mannequin holding a rug with Nancy in the foreground. The Turkish girl in the story was named Aisha, which was almost like my name. Nancy had gushed over her dark hair and eyes, which were like mine. Aisha had long hair, while mine was chopped short, à la Dorothy Hamill. However, that was closer to me than Nancy's blond perfectly flipped hair. I recall references to a bracelet or a ring made of gold filigree. This reminded me of all the Indian gold hoops that I wore daily and wasn't allowed to remove.

I devoured that book a few times because I was so excited by this dark-haired Aisha, one that bewitched our own Nancy. There was a fascinating narrative, in which I learned about the power of rugs as conduits of coded messages. Most of the information about the Turkish culture was straightforward, and, without a doubt, this intrigued Nancy. There are swarthy and shadowy men, and a sudden trip to Istanbul. Nancy was cool about everything, and stayed focused on her mission.

As I mentioned, this was the 1970s, before Priyanka Chopra and Mindy Kaling graced network TV, or anyone even entertained a minor character like Parvati Patil as a Hogwarts student. It was hard to find myself or my culture acknowledged in conventional American books and movies. The only references we saw in books were to Mahatma Gandhi, Indira Gandhi, or Mother Teresa, and most mainstream movies were period pieces during the British occupation of India.

Nancy Drew hardly falls under the category of "multicultural fiction," and we could probably comb through it with twenty-first century sensibilities about cultural stereotypes. However, *Mysterious Mannequin* stood out as Nancy dared to dive into different cultures. Carolyn Keene handled this well and attempted to be informative. There is an openness in Nancy that made her more appealing as she dove into this foreign culture and community. For a young girl, a story like this sets the subconscious notion that if Nancy were real, maybe we could be friends. I could introduce her to my world too.

PAUL FERICANO

My Prom Date with Nancy Drew

Ever since you can remember
he comes through the front door
hat in hand both arms outstretched
greets you the same way every night
solve any mysteries lately?
Then laughs big and broad
and musses your hair
and lifts you on his knee
the one with shrapnel from the war
limping and dragging his shadow
like Chester in *Gunsmoke*
and prompting all his friends to ask
how's Mr. Dillon?

It's strange to think of this now
eager and anxious
ringing your doorbell
corsage in a pink box under arm
meeting him for the first time
standing with pipe in one hand
newspaper in the other
studying me in my white sport coat
my polished wingtips
asking *which Hardy are you? Frank or Joe?*
And me with a dumb quizzical look
in the glow of a yellow porch light
wondering what to say
And you standing next to him
hair up shimmering in blue formal
rolling your eyes and smiling

LINDA McCAULEY FREEMAN

A Clue

Nancy drew far more
than she knew

the bright yellow
book bindings

unbound
her hair her brain

she always knew
to look beyond

better than anyone
she gave me

a clue for how
to live my life

unbound.

VIJAYA GOWRISANKAR

Darkness now intrigues

Glow of light a constant companion
For darkness was a frightening feeling
From streetlights to night lamps to stars
Or a torch that I always carried as armor
Or tightly clasped hands of elders as support
This defined me for the first ten years of life

Nancy Drew then crept in, to replace Enid Blyton books
Fingernails chewed as each page unraveled her strength
Sleepless nights where darkness was forgotten
As mind grappled with the plot of each mystery
Each book left me yearning for more, filled with awe
She became an inseparable part of my life and thoughts

An invisible friend, not an imaginary fictional character
She brought about subtle changes in my personality
My walk was more confident, fear fled to find another victim
I was more alert of my surroundings, no longer a shrinking violet
Looking at life and people with a different perspective
My parents smiled secretly at this transformation by Nancy Drew

Geosi Gyasi

Speech & Prize-Giving Day
Inspired by *The Quest of the Missing Map*

After the speech & prize-giving day, I opened the prize. Winning the first prize in math was no mean feat. You would understand why. The numbers speak for themselves. Out of two hundred students in class, I was the top. But I was weak in other subjects too. Particularly, English, where the teacher bothered us with tons and tons of classics. Shakespeare, Chaucer, Tolstoy, you name them. I opened the prize to find a surprise. A storybook. That was the prize. Nothing more. Nothing less. What was a top student in math going to do with a Nancy Drew book? I gave the book a befitting burial. Inside my box, I hid it in a cloud of darkness. Never to see it again until the time of resurrection. When I met Nancy at page one, she held my arms through a journey. With unexpected twists and turns. I was afraid like Ellen Smith who was offered a job to teach piano lessons. At the mysterious place of Rocky Edge. I held my breath at page eight. When Nancy entered the abandoned one-room cottage. The map and the buried treasure quickly came to mind. I was scared for Nancy's life. Eager to know what would happen next.

MAUREEN HADZICK-SPISAK

Ninety-Nine Cents

It doesn't seem like much today
Ninety-nine cents
For a book that was fulfilling my dreams
Guiding my life
Nancy Drew was every girl's fantasy
Rich, attractive, and clever
The epitome of style and daring
Week after week
I saved my quarter allowance
When I had that dollar
I raced down Haspel Hill
Up Grand Avenue to the
Nearest Five and Dime
Praying they would have
Nancy's latest mystery
Once back in my room
Nancy and I began our newest adventure
We searched for clues in
Hidden staircases, under Larkspur bushes
And even old clocks
We went on midnight watches
Praying our flashlight would stay lit
She never disappointed me
As I reached the end
I slowed down wishing it
Would never end

JESSIE KEARY

Murder-Suicide: Nancy Drew and Me

In the conservatory of Blackmoor Manor, there is a giant carnivorous plant. You see the plant through Nancy's eyes. You are nothing but a suggestion in her head. With a click, you tell her to touch the waxen leaves. She says, "I don't think that's a good idea." You tell her to do it anyway. With no leads or cheats, you are bored, and her life is your game. Your wireless mouse pulls her like puppet strings. She submits with two more clicks.

Her scream rips through your childhood chapter books gathering dust. Your mouth falls open, hand hovering over mouse, the murder weapon. You stare at Nancy's legs sticking straight up from the plant. She is wearing purple pumps. The screen goes black. You don't blink. You didn't think anyone could kill Nancy Drew until you did. You deny the darkness within you, just like everyone else. It was an accident.

Would you like a second chance? You take it, even though you know you will never beat a Nancy Drew game. You can't beat Nancy at her own game. You can try seeing the world from her point of view, but her thoughts are not like yours. She's all go-getter, forward thinker. You are stuck on a downbeat. When you call the Hardy Boys, desperate for a tip, it goes straight to voicemail. Nancy figures everything out. All that runs through your mind is the obligation to keep playing. You need more to enjoy the game. You walk Nancy back to the conservatory and click on the carnivorous plant until you run out of second chances.

GAME OVER

MARK HUDSON

The Secret of the Old Clock

The Secret of the Old Clock
Nancy Drew number one #16
Interpreted by Mark Hudson 2016

ELIZABETH KERPER

Nancy Drew Can't Help Me

In the empty wooded lot behind my house there was a tractor tire,
toppled, weeds rippling up through the treads, a sapling sprouting
in its empty center, and the crossbeam and posts of a swing set
left to rot, and once even two white-tailed deer crossing the patch
of thorny brush beside the megachurch in a pair of parabola leaps,
but never a band of jewel thieves, never a crumbling wall
with the scraps of a treasure map wedged between stones and mortar,
never a flicker of light glimpsed late at night giving me just the clue

I needed. Nancy makes pirouette turns in her powder blue roadster
while I failed the driving test the first time, at eighteen, after two years
of letting everyone assume I had already passed. I don't know semaphore
or fencing or French or how to cross my wrists as they're tied so the ropes
won't hold, don't own a tasteful navy suit or a single pair of pumps. Nancy
feels pure satisfaction, I assume, when the case is closed, her sleuthing
successful, the wallpaper stripped away from truth's hidden door,
never feels a twinge of loss when potential contracts into absolute, and yes,
there are times when I too long to trade the mysteries I can't solve
for ones I can, but I know that this is not how character gets developed,
that Nancy has so many skills for a girl who will never turn nineteen.

JOAN LEOTTA

Get a Clue!

Nancy Drew as a source of inspiration, now, as well as then!
It never mattered to me that Carolyn Keene was not just one person—
It's the heroine Nancy who held me in thrall and still acts as muse.
A bit of a rhyme

Nowadays, when fighting writers block,
when working up against the clock

scribbling my plot without a clue
as to what hero or villain should do,
when breaking for tea and cookie just won't do,
I seek inspiration from Nancy Drew.

I open a volume from my childhood friend
rereading how *she* brought plots to an end.
She now oft whispers how my books should trend
After all, she started me writing, even then.

In her company I tracked and spied
imaginary evildoers with nine lives.
So, I still use her help to work and devise
plots that amuse—after many tries.

My writings today are more diverse,
sometimes long, sometimes terse—
articles, shorts, books, even verse
But thru all she remains my writing muse.

When my own writing is done,
I pull out her books, (don't own *every* one).
As I settle back to reread a tome
or to write, it's Nancy creed drives me on

"Forward, forward, find those clues!"
Ah, how much I owe to my Nancy Drews!

SHAHÉ MANKERIAN

Dear 12-Year-Old Self

Ride your bicycle a lot.
Don't pick up magazines
in the alley. Don't call

any of the girls. Samantha
does not exist. Her phone
number belongs to Tyrone.

If you want to talk
to girls, go to the library.
The girl sitting pretzel style

in the Nancy Drew aisle
might be shy, but talk to her.
She will know more

about boys than Samantha
or Tyrone. Carry the books
she checked out to her bike.

Memorize the titles
because your job is to know
Nancy Drew. After you watch

her ride off into the sunset,
run to the checkout desk,
and apply for a library card.

CATHY MCARTHUR

Nine Years Old: Nancy Drew

All summer I open books, keep
The Secret of the Old Clock
in my room

I know *The Password*
to Larkspur Lane
at night hold a flashlight

to *The Hidden Staircase*
and *Nancy's Mysterious Letter*
while everyone in the house sleeps.

I pick up *A Clue In the Diary*
carry *The Mystery*
of The Ivory Charm

know the whole story
in my room
in the back of the house.

All summer the fan hums.
I find and keep *The Secret*
of The Wooden Lady,

read by my open window
The Message
in the Hollow Oak.

NANCY MCCABE

Coming of Age with Nancy Drew

I first started reading Nancy Drew because my cousin Jody did. I was always trying, mostly unsuccessfully, to keep up with Jody, and by the time I cracked open my first Nancy Drew, she had moved on to Agatha Christie. It annoyed me the way she regularly talked about Miss Marple and Hercule Poirot as if they were real people. I felt left behind now that she had crossed an invisible line from the mild thefts, scams, and lost inheritances of children's mysteries to the gritty murders and sly deceptions of adult books.

But Nancy Drew was all I could handle. I found the stories so vivid, tense, and claustrophobic that I had nightmares. Yet I continued to read them, sucked into their alluring details: mansions, prisoners in towers, buried treasure chests, orphans of unknown parentage, doubles, phantom ships and horses, frightful howls and bloodcurdling screams. I was lured by bats, dust, cobwebs, old diaries and lockets and moldering wardrobes, tunnels and secret cupboards and compartments, loose bricks and panels and floorboards, whatever could hold secrets. In climactic moments, Nancy is tied up on a sinking ship and left to drown, bound and gagged and tossed into a hidden underground room à la Edgar Allan Poe, threatened with confinement in closets, caves, tunnels. "You'll never see daylight again," the villains like to declare.

I spent most of my allowance at Kmart on the yellow-spined hardcovers, what I later found out were Nancy's second incarnation, because I couldn't find the books at the library. When I finally inquired why not, a librarian gently told me that Nancy Drews were not good literature. There was no actual Carolyn Keene; the books had no real author. They were produced by a syndicate, a sort of book factory, where the boss wrote an outline according to a formula, and then an employee fleshed out the story. Then another one edited it so it would sound like all the others, and ta-da, a book was born.

My family regularly visited Henry's candy factory in Dexter, Kansas. There, we watched workers stirring, pouring, turning, peeling, and cutting the hard candy, cleanly, expertly, relaxed but efficient, perfectly in sync. When I tried to picture a writing factory, Henry's was my only frame of reference. I envisioned a huge room full of metal tables, some filled with writers madly scribbling Hardy Boys stories, others frowning thoughtfully as they edited new Bobbsey Twins books.

In the Nancy Drew row of my imagination, the boss finished dashing off an outline and passed it to the detail filler. Titian hair, check. Blue convertible, check. On down the line to a researcher: a lesser-known name for lilacs is blue pipes. Insert paragraph. On to another writer: suspenseful climax involving confinement. Finally, to the writer who produced the last page, which always alluded to the next mystery: "During the discussion, Nancy was wondering what her next mystery would be. It was a puzzling one, which was called *Password to Larkspur Lane*."

My image of assembly-line book creation secretly inspired me. I pictured how, at the end of the day, all the writers would throw down their pens in satisfaction, yawning and stretching and buzzing about the recent plot developments. I envied the imagined camaraderie between syndicate writers. I wanted a job like that someday.

I didn't need to believe in Carolyn Keene to love Nancy Drew any more than I needed to believe in Betty Crocker to enjoy cake. But the librarian's words planted a seed of doubt. I generally liked to picture the authors of my favorite books as real people, grown up versions of Harriett, Heidi, Anne, Laura. But Nancy had never seemed real enough for me to envision her as Carolyn Keene's thinly disguised younger self. I never once imagined a grown woman giving up a leisurely, adventurous, and fashionable life of sleuthing to sit typing all day in her olive-green knit with matching shoes and beige accessories. And I hadn't yet internalized the expectation that a single author should function as the center of authority. Nor did I have any notion that ghostwriters or collaborative processes might be regarded as violations of public trust or compromises of artistic integrity.

Still, my niggling doubt took hold and I began to find fault with Nancy Drew. I noticed that her hair was sometimes blond, sometimes "titian," which my dad said was more reddish, strawberry blond, after the favorite models of a famous painter. The inconsistency made me wonder if the syndicate was always on its toes. And then *The Clue of the Broken Locket* described a boy and girl as "identical twins," a sentence on which I heaped all of my twelve-year-old scorn. Even I knew that a boy and girl could only be fraternal twins.

And now the floodgates opened. I became more and more annoyed by Nancy's perfection, something for which other readers admired her. The healing powers of girls' book heroines, the dazzling competence of Pa Ingalls, combined anew in the character of Nancy Drew. Nothing fazed her. If someone at a neighboring table choked on raw steak, she paused from tracing clues to administer the Heimlich, add a delicious marinade to the meat, and fire up her portable grill to ensure that it was fully cooked. If Nancy's boyfriend Ned discovered a message in hieroglyphics, Nancy darted over to translate it—into French by way of Swahili. If her car overheated, Nancy purchased a new thermostat and installed it herself, substituting roadside sticks and rocks for more conventional tools. If Nancy's slacks ripped while she was camping on a mountainside, she whipped out her sewing kit and stitched up a pair of new pants from tent cloth. So maybe these are exaggerations of Nancy's prowess—but not by much.

Nancy was the original Barbie, thin and stylish and endlessly versatile, capable of assuming a new role with each new outfit, a short cultural leap to Newborn Baby Doctor Barbie, Aerospace Engineer Barbie, Sea World Trainer Barbie, and Beach Party Barbie. But just as I never got into Barbie, Nancy was too relentlessly competent for my taste. She was effortlessly attractive, kind, and skillful, and we were repeatedly told how modest she was, even though she was always introducing herself by saying things like, "I'm Nancy Drew. My father is Carson Drew, the attorney." Those words smacked to me of privilege and entitlement, an expectation that everyone should have heard of and been impressed by her father.

Sharing her first name called attention to all that I could not live up to. In contrast to the young sleuth, I was shy and awkward, and my world felt out of my control. In real life, modesty and shyness came down to the same thing, rendering me invisible. Nancy got away with so much; it wasn't fair. She observed the faint sound of crickets on a pirated recording and concluded that it had been made at Pudding Stone Lodge because you could hear crickets there at night. I railed at this ludicrous deduction: where couldn't you hear crickets at night?

My concept of how the world worked, with God in his heaven, the righteous vindicated, and truth and justice prevailing, was beginning to erode.

"I'm getting tired of Nancy Drew," I told my mother. "The books are all the same." Once I'd become attuned to the pattern of each plot, it became glaringly obvious how alike they were.

Mom nodded sagely. "You've discovered the difference between good literature and trash," she said.

I felt vaguely duped, as if Nancy Drew were my own personal emblem of receding innocence. I went overboard, trying to get back at what? A fictional character? A fictional author? A publishing industry that had tricked me? I started writing my own Nancy Drew stories full of absurdities, meant to be acerbically witty.

Santa Claus is a central figure in my first Nancy Drew story, "Mystery at the North Pole," in which the girl detective heads off to assist the "jolly old elf" with an unspecified problem. I mostly included Santa Claus because it seemed so ridiculous, but now I realize that he's Carolyn Keene multiplied exponentially, the ultimate cultural deception, the elemental representative of mystical childhood belief debunked.

Furthermore, he's a benign figure on the surface, but beneath it all, not so different from your average creepy criminal.

His methodology involves peeping and stalking—he sees you when you're sleeping? He knows when you're awake?—and breaking and entering. Granted, he leaves stuff instead of taking it, but still embedded in the whole Santa Claus myth is an acceptance of violation and intrusion if performed by the right well-intentioned cultural construction.

So there you have it, my twelve-year-old disillusionment in a nutshell: Santa Claus didn't exist, Carolyn Keene didn't exist, crime isn't always punished, there is evil in us all. And so I went for the jugular as best I knew how, attacking the weaknesses of plot and character in the books that stood for all that had betrayed me.

Eventually, after five or so ruthlessly ridiculous but unfinished Nancy Drew stories of my own, I spent my rage. But it was a long time before I would grudgingly give her credit for being a model of independence and daring who may not have consciously recast femininity for me but who did, in a roundabout way, help make me a writer. And sometimes what kept me going in grad school was feeling like Nancy Drew in a land of meanings to be uncovered, processes and influences to be discovered.

When I returned to Nancy Drew after a hiatus of many years, I found myself sucked right back in. My daughter and I started playing Nancy Drew computer games when she was eight, and eventually solved twelve of them, albeit only on the junior level. In these games, we became Nancy Drew, questioning suspects, solving puzzles, completing tasks. My rage toward Nancy mellowed; I'd softened; or maybe I was just less resentful because the game required me to be the competent one. Besides, if Nancy got too annoying, we could have her poison the horses and get her kicked off of Shadow Ranch, blow up the boiler room and have her thrown from River Heights High School, or feed her to a man-eating plant in Blackmoor Manor. There was a mechanism for second chances, and third, and fourth, and fifth, so we could kill off Nancy repeatedly, then revive her and re-enter the game.

It was very satisfying. Now I was the powerful one.

PATRICIA MCGOLDRICK

Secrets and Clues and Mysteries, Oh My!

I first met Nancy Drew at the local public library. Well, actually, at the age of ten, our local war-bride librarian, Mrs. C., introduced me to the mystery-solving character of Nancy Drew.

Thanks to this cheerful English woman, the Grand Valley Carnegie Public Library was a well-stocked collection for all ages in our rural community. Before the Internet revolution, my friends and I were guided, by this local librarian, along a reading path that took us on many journeys, far beyond the farms and small villages in Canada where we lived.

Nancy Drew and her escapades quickly became a favorite series as we followed her through a maze of secrets, clues, and mysteries. Beginning with *The Secret of the Old Clock* through to *The Thirteenth Pearl,* we accompanied Nancy on her adventures.

We didn't belong to a formal book blub. Avid readers, five of us in all, we just shared thoughts about the stories we'd read—favorite aspects and others not so much.

Our loose network of friends became amateur sleuths as we followed along with the strong, female character in the numerous stories. As young girls, we were drawn to the problem-solving heroine, Nancy Drew.

In the mid-sixties, as we read through the series, the titles piqued our interest. Words such as secret, clue, sign, password, haunted, quest, invited us to delve into these books to solve the latest mystery.

Weekly, we visited the library shelves to obtain another Nancy Drew edition. Each book had an envelope pocket in it that contained a sign-up card for borrowers. Eventually, our group of five was represented on each of these Nancy Drew book cards.

As we finished these Nancy Drew volumes, we looked to Mrs. C. for another recommendation. She did not disappoint, "No question, girls! Next check out The Hardy Boys, and then you'll be ready for Mary Stewart!"

MICHELLE MCMILLAN-HOLIFIELD

Quest of the Missing _____

Nancy Drew #19 Quest of the Missing Map: First "adult" book
I read completely by myself cover to cover, no help. Third
grade. As I turned that last page, a sensation overcame me that
I could not put into words at the time, but what I now recognize
as satiety, accomplishment. I swung my pajamaed legs over the
side of my bed and, book in hand, one eye lingering on those
last few words, skipped through the house. Quest: my mother's
approval. I proclaimed my emphatic *Guess what?* and pirouet-
ted, pliéd, as I leapt into her lap. She knew my success. My in-
tellect never a mystery to this woman.

My mother read the first 18 Nancy Drews aloud to me. Her de-
votion stirs me. Makes me wish I could have children so I
could devote my nights to reading aloud to them a few chapters
a night, while their sweaty little heads rest on my shoulder.
Embolden their sense of adventure. Look up words we don't
recognize. Do all women want children this badly or is it just
the women who can't have them? In all my medical records,
the reason for my infertility eludes me.

There are no answers, Nancy. Not to this mystery. My body
has been examined. The microscope, the magnifying glass, all
manner of invasive instruments—they've all been sleuths on
the case. And I wish I could call you in, turn the case over to
you, present you with the evidence: ultrasounds highlighting
oddities in my ovaries, calendars where I've mapped out my
cycles and counted the days from one set of pills to the next,
the + or − tests. All. Failed. You work out the symbols in my
mysterious ultrasonic photographs, and I'll nurse the fractures
webbing inside my heart. ⟩

In sixth grade, my mother would not let me spend the night with a friend, so while she chatted with my friend's mother, I slammed my elbow through her truck window. This was an accident on purpose. What I mean is I purposely elbowed the window, but I had no clue it was weak enough to shatter at my rage. I thought: *I'm jinxed. I'm caught.* I lied, cried, told my mother I slammed the door too hard. Never mind the large hole surrounded by a web of hairline fractures. Never mind the trail of blood down my arm that started at my elbow. My mother: on the case. I was questioned. I lied and lied then later signed my confession in a letter I left on the table as she slept. My savings account was confiscated. All one hundred and twenty three dollars.

Is it a sin I have not confessed? Has the blessing of children been confiscated? Did I curse myself somehow? I confess that in my twenties I claimed I did not want children. And I have confessed that confession before God, aloud, and begged forgiveness. I am an only child, my mother's one chance to have grandchildren; I carry my guilt like a too-heavy purse I can't seem to put down. That yoke (I put it on myself) is burdensome. I confess I am not as good a sleuth as my mother: I haven't been able to glean from the nuance of her voice how she feels to have a daughter who is less. Childless, less than a woman. An unsuccess.

❖

Nancy, you are motherless. Does it feel the same as this: broken, fractured, jinxed? You are missing a mother; I'm missing a child. Did you leave clues in a secret diary? Did you confess you missed what was missing so much you splayed your body face down on the bed and let your screams soak the sheets? I confess I miss curling up in my mother's lap, laying my sweaty head on her shoulder as she read and read until all the mysteries were solved. Quest: questions answered. Quest: to conceive a child would be as simple as conceiving *of* a child. Quest: to be less childless.

CAROLINA MORALES

In Nancy Drew's shadow

From the white & black of printed pages
to the black & white of our first TV
where the mystery of shadows trailed
the shadow of a mystery, I followed
her plotted path, book to screen then
screen to book, each latest case
for a teenage sleuth to muse & solve.
X marks the spot—in the blue sky world
where a blue-eyed girl owns her own
sky blue car, a housekeeper keeps
a tidy house, a father installed
in his study smoking his pipe
far from the pipe fittings, the smoke stacks
of a factory town, a ramshackle house,
a room overshadowed by factory walls,
a window foreshadowed by gray light,
night smoking into light gray
stack pipes smoking into the night,
a crowded sill of dusty pages,
a dusty screen on a crowded shelf
where a dark-eyed girl who had no father
followed the trail of a motherless teen
through the pages of *The Crumbling Wall*
to the wall crumbling on the small screen.
Too young to follow behind my mother
into the shadow of the factory gate,
I remained a shadow sister
scripted towards a shadow fate.

LYLANNE MUSSELMAN

Solving Mysteries

I barely remember Bess Marvin,
or Ned Nickerson, the token
boy. Alliteration was all
he was good for. Nothing
in my eyes, could top

> *The Mystery of the 99 Steps,*
and adventures with George,
except the 42 volumes
that came before, in my books,

read over and over again;
I spent so many hours
with you, teaching me:
> *girls could be cool,*
> *independent, smart,*
> *always solving clues—*

me dreaming of being like you,
or your hero sidekick; swapping
secrets with my favorite sleuth:
> *Nancy Drew.*

FAYE PANTAZOPOULOS

Buried Secrets

I've always been curious,
questioning,
in search of secrets ...
I was sure the adults were
keeping from me.
I channeled Nancy Drew at 7,
hiding in the hallway closet
when they thought I was in bed
asleep.
I waited, and waited . . . the door slightly ajar—
my first stakeout—
until I saw my father placing
gifts under the Christmas tree.
I knew it!
There was no Santa, just as my classmate said.
It was the first mystery I ever solved . . .
and there was no stopping me afterwards.
I was always imitating that titian-haired
teenage detective,
staying indoors at recess to sleuth
around the school,
bossing Bess and George around.
My mind was sharp and always
seeking the hidden truth.
Today I know better.
There are many truths
and I know where they're buried,
but it's best to not dig them up.

STEPHANIE R. PEARMAIN

My Nancy Drew

Burning beds
Colonial houses with ghosts, spiders' webs, and secrets
Waiting to be discovered.

A quest through dark, echoing library halls
After an eclectic fieldtrip to a hole-in-the-wall bookshop
To purchase the *Egyptian Book of the Dead.*

Old clocks
That tick like whispers telling the secret of time
While it continues slipping away too silently to hear.

Summer at the pool,
The dewy smell of dawn at the beach
And the promise of endless playful, sunny days.

A record player
Spinning eerie songs beneath a window pried open,
The scent of lilac sneaking in.

The sound of vinyl
And Dad's footsteps upstairs,
The crackling soundtrack of carefree, lazy days.

Mystery
And piercing screams,
Cliffside caves and hidden stairs.

A maze of tunnel-like paths
Meandering through a childhood when hours still seemed like
     days.
Made up stories in a diary, kept in the safety of the locket
     that is my heart.

A bridge haunted by inevitable truths,
  The crumbling walls of childhood
    Reveal stolen gems and lost telegrams,

A trunk of treasured memories resurfacing
  Beneath a sun casting rays over the dark shadows,
    Giving rise to a woman who stands waving goodbye,

Holding a bright yellow bookmark of
  hieroglyph etchings and a dusty old book
    with a beautifully faded yellow spine.

ANNA PESNELL

Nancy Made Me What I Am Today

If I could meet any person, I would choose Edward Strate-meyer, an author who helped pave the way for kids' fiction. His character of Nancy Drew is a large part of why I became interested in reading. I began reading Nancy Drew books when I was in second grade. I've been hooked ever since. Nancy Drew has been my idol for years, and if I could meet the man who created her, I would thank him for making my childhood reading experience wonderful.

I attribute most of my good qualities to having read a lot as a child. I devoured books. Even though I don't have as much time to read now, I still enjoy it. I feel that without Nancy Drew Mystery Stories, I may not have found a series that grabbed my interest and held it for so many years. Because the series is so extensive and is still expanding, I never ran out of material. I read book after book, adventuring with the characters that Stratemeyer created and that ghostwriters under the pseudonym Carolyn Keene keep alive even today.

Edward Stratemeyer founded a syndicate of writers and specifically set out to produce books for children that were not just for moral instruction. He realized that there was a world of opportunity that was still undiscovered. He wanted to make books that children could read for entertainment. With his syndicate, he created The Hardy Boys, The Bobbsey Twins, and, of course, Nancy Drew. He and his daughters, Harriet and Edna, made plot outlines for ghostwriters to use as a basis for each story. This is how they managed to make so many volumes of one series. There are several other series besides the original Nancy Drew Mystery Stories, including The Nancy Drew Diaries, The Nancy Drew Files, and Girl Detective, all of which I have sampled.

My love of reading has expanded to other genres besides mysteries. However, mystery stories will always be my favorite.

I have Edward Stratemeyer and his syndicate to thank for that. I now own at least fifty volumes, a variety of collectors' items, and multiple PC games. I have two bookshelves set aside specifically for Nancy Drew books and other mystery novels. As I previously stated, I believe that if it were not for Stratemeyer and his creation of this iconic character, I would not be the person I am today.

Anna Pesnell relaxes on a hammock while reading *The Secret of the Old Clock* (New York: Grosset & Dunlap, 1930)—with other books in her Nancy Drew collection close at hand.

JESSICA PURDY

Mystery

I wanted to be a detective, a private eye.
I would lie on the blue corduroy
couch and read Nancy
Drew while nibbling on a cherry
chapstick. I wore a costume jewelry
emerald bracelet whose eye shape affected me deeply
when it reflected the green light of day.
The idea of trapdoors consumed my
imagination. I wanted a secret staircase, a spy
code, a hiding place beneath a loose board, a box filled with spidery
handwriting found in a gully.
My sister loved paper dolls of famous royalty.
I envied her knowledge of beheaded women and their finery,
but their dresses dripped with dislocation. They had nothing to do with me. Every
old thing I found was a clue, even if it was miscellany.
Once I spent the entirety
of an afternoon trespassing on the neighbor's abandoned property
where I pieced together newspaper clippings, tools, insect shells, and toys,
certain I would uncover the truth. Mysteries where there were none. Bravery.
Evidence is objects in eternity.
Here is what you cannot know. Now solve for y.

CYNTHIA TODD QUAM

What Nancy Drew

Carolyn lied to little girls,
wrote Nancy blonde in one book,
red-haired in another,
swore (without four-letter words)
that natural curls and yellow roadsters
aren't hereditary,

claimed a girl could hail a safe cab
or the Hardy Boys,
pick any man's lock with a hairpin
and stay pure.

too late we learn
The Secret of the Old Clock
is simply that it keeps on ticking,
know the mysterious voice on the wire
as our own, thirty years from now,

ringing back to remind us
as we scribble clues
on the bent backs of old envelopes,
to turn them over, please,
and check the postmark.

STEPHEN D. ROGERS

The Case of the Immortal Detective

Nancy not only links clues
But generations
My mother read the books to me
I read them to my daughter
She may read them to her own
All of us following Nancy
As Nancy solves the case

SHEIKHA A.

Locked

"There are some doors that should never be opened."

Maybe if there were a dragon
hidden in my closet of secrets,
would I say to it:

right, let's solve your mystery!

would it be brave to double up
gather my lock picks and pins
under a clever blue cap of ideas
and march out to mission;

would that make me closer
to knowing how the dragon came
to fit in my cluttered dominion
of slim but sure evidence;

would its mouth open
to reveal all its plans—
there is a mystery, like Nancy
that crops up everywhere I go—

close calls of bold resourcefulness,
a second way should open through
for the dragon didn't just drop in
from the chimney chute;

the clock's nightly echoes
beckon the existence of a second door

there are too many puzzles
too many mysteries

it's locked! ➢

my mother's voice of reason chimes:
for how long does a person's curiosity
keep them sane / safe, or maybe sage
Nancy knows better than I:

"There are some doors that hold secrets that should never be known."

DOROTHY SWOOPE

You'll Ruin Your Eyes

Dottie!

Mom's voice reached me from outside my makeshift tent of covers where I was surreptitiously reading by flashlight after "lights out." I was near the end of an exciting Nancy Drew mystery. Nancy had just discovered the missing dancer who stood to inherit the castle and they were both in danger. I couldn't stop now.

It's 11 o'clock and you've got school tomorrow.

But I'm nearly finished, just a little more . . .

Give me that flashlight. The beam of light caught Mom's features in a weird ghoulish light. It was rare for my mother to look menacing but she did now.

Don't shine it in my eyes! She grabbed the flashlight and turned the beam on me. *Hand over the book.*

Mom, I pleaded, knowing it was lost.

Dottie.

I reluctantly handed over *The Clue in the Crumbling Wall.* Now I would toss and turn all night imagining the worst, wondering what happened in the end. I know Nancy always came out unscathed but it was a close call. Right up to the last page, you could never figure out how she was going to escape and solve the crime. I loved reading. It removed me from the ordinariness of my life on Hillcrest Avenue.

The next morning I slept in. Mom was not impressed and it just reaffirmed her rules about not staying up late reading. So I had to wait until the end of the day to finish my book. It was torture.

Thank goodness it was Friday and the next day was *no school* Saturday.

I felt a surge of excitement when I woke up. Usually Saturday mornings were laden with chores before anything exciting could happen. Dusting and cleaning were the usual or, depending on the season, the dreaded yard work such as autumn leaf raking. At any moment over the weekend our father could decide to muster the troops for a foray into the backyard, unless of course there was snow on the ground.

Digging out dandelions was the worst job, grubbing in the dirt, exposing disgusting, wriggling worms, wearing my soft hands into tiny painful blisters. I would rather be daydreaming with a book, immersing myself into an exciting life, solving mysteries with Nancy or saving lives like nurse, Clara Barton. My penchant for romance at that stage was chaste but I was big on hero/heroine worship.

The earliest books I remember reading myself, were the Bobbsey Twins' series of adventures. I wanted to be a twin. I imagined having someone just like me always there and really nice to be with, unlike my tortuous older brother, Richard, or my pesky younger brother, Bobby. (My older sister, Sandy, was far too mature to bother with me unless it was to her advantage.) Reading curbed my loneliness, let me loose in another world, a more exciting world than mine.

When I wasn't reading, I was watching Fred Astaire and Ginger Rogers in the ultimate glamorous sweep around the dance floor. Ginger wore a daring backless, full-length pleated chiffon dress with a feathered hem that rippled around her high-heeled feet, dancing backwards in intricate maneuvers to Fred's lead. I could only imagine the glorious colors as TV came only in black and white then.

I lived in a world of daydreams. I was a fabulous dancer, I had gorgeous designer clothes and could lounge around all day long, planning which ball gown I'd wear that night. I spent hours re-enacting such scenes with my paper dolls. Veronica was my favorite paper doll. She was almost as glamorous as Ginger, only she had brown hair. I made fancy gowns out of paper for her with shoulder tabs to attach them. I spent hours of pleasure, creating the perfect outfit for an exciting event. Hollywood dreams permeated our living room every day, in my mind at least.

But reading was the perfect escape. No one changed the channel on you at that critical moment. I would have been happy reading all day everyday. But cleaning was a set Saturday morning thing, and we all had to pitch in. Saturday cleaning chores could last all day if a holiday was looming. Then I was stuck polishing the silver—a satisfying enough job but it left my hands dry and flaky. Dusting made me sneeze, but it didn't get me out of the job. Before too long I'd be humming along to *The Nutcracker Suite* with my mother, gliding through the morning until all the timber surfaces gleamed and the cobwebs were banished.

This Saturday I was excited because we were going to the library. It was a ritual my father organized every couple of weeks. I gathered all the books from my previous visit, some to renew, but mostly they were all read—and I was looking forward to Nancy's next adventure.

We drove the mile into town from Burnham Park. Carrying an armload of books up the hill was not appealing. The library was off the Green in the older part of town, part of a cluster of grand buildings from another time. It was next to the oldest bank with its grand columns and the theatre in a similar Georgian style. Around the corner was the Ford Mansion, where George Washington stayed the winter of 1779-1780. The Continental Army camped at Jockey Hollow and a group of the men built Fort Nonsense, where on a clear day you would see the red coats of the British crossing the river into New Jersey from New York City. The library was more in the Greek revival style, built in of gray stone with an imposing golden dome over the circular section.

It took my breath away to walk into that golden-ceilinged foyer. It was so different from my everyday world with its patterned-marble floor and ornate, curved ceiling. Busts of the great philosophers and a giant golden eagle greeted you. Then there were layers and layers of books. Looking up to where only adults could go, I longed for that day, said goodbye to my father as we returned our books at the counter and went our separate ways.

He left me to browse at my leisure in the children's wing and would often seek me out lost, behind the mountain of books I juggled while still looking for more. It was exciting, obsessive. And then of course once I got home, all I wanted to do was read.

Dad would settle into the "fuzzy" chair with his feet propped up on the hassock, a bowl of peanuts at hand. He would read until the book fell gently into his lap and a buzz-saw snore emitted from his relaxed face. *Just resting my eyes,* he'd say on waking with a start. You could never get away with pinching peanuts. He was such a light sleeper. If he fell asleep watching baseball, and you were desperate to watch Cary Grant and Katharine Hepburn on the other channel, you had no chance. Just go near the TV and he'd bark.

I'm watching that! I was just resting my eyes. It was like radar.

Tucked up in my eaved bedroom, pillows fluffed around me, I was straining with the afternoon light to see, when my mother's voice broke my concentration.

Put the light on. You'll ruin your eyes. (How many times had I heard that?) *Supper's almost ready. Come and set the table.*

I'll be right there, I'll just finish . . .

Now!

Unfair, I thought as I placed the paper doll bookmark in my book. She could have at least let me get to the end of the chapter.

SHREHYA TANEJA

Nancy in India

Was a collection of books
Secondhand and yellowing
'Cause of the constant borrowing
The pavements with
Stocked and returned titles
Or the huge bookshop
Begging my mother
To let me buy one more
And enter into her adventures
Unknown to me
A girl she seemed
With friends who stayed
Next door
Separated by ages
Of mass culture
And a nation
To me that
Had no relation
Nancy made a connection
Her independence
Quirkiness and her own den
Her inquisitive profession
Inspired a vivid memory
Made the eyes of a
Small Indian girl light up
And start dreaming
When she was surrounded by
Her aunt's wedding preparations
She pored over Nancy and Ned
George and Bess
Traveling and rafting
A childhood desire resurrected
Of being another
Nancy

MARJORIE TESSER

Girl Sleuth

Jill and Bridget find reading boring, but Annie secretly loves to disappear into a book. Her favorite is Nancy Drew. Ever since her older cousin Barbara passed her copies along to her, Annie has devoured as many volumes as she can get her hands on. Her cousin's copies are faded blue, and in them Nancy has crimped hair and wears long tailored suits, like in an old fashioned movie. In the newer books with the yellow and blue covers she has a flip and dresses like a normal girl in a shirtwaist. Annie is particularly interested in the milieu and the language of the books, so different from the way people act and talk in her Brooklyn neighborhood. Carson Drew is a "prominent attorney," not just a lawyer, like Uncle Howie. Nancy and her friends drive "roadsters" and "coupés," not plain sedans like Annie's dad. When Hannah Gruen, Nancy's pleasant but unbossy housekeeper, goes to bed, she "retires" (when Annie first read this, she thought Hannah had really retired, stopped working, and she worried who would take care of Nancy. She finally figured it out when Hannah appeared, still baking muffins, later in the book). Annie covets the life of a girl detective—a *sleuth*, as the books call it—so different from her normal world. Her dad would pretty much let her do what she wanted. She'd have interesting friends who didn't make fun of her or call her a baby, ever, one fluffy, one sporty, like Bess and George. She'd drive her own cute blue car. She'd have a boyfriend, not exactly like Ned, who seems kind of bland and preppy, but someone cuter, like Tommy Fusco. Hiding out, unafraid, in the old mill or the attic or the spooky house and catching the bandits red-handed sounds like the perfect job for Annie. Annie would be brave and smart. She would figure it all out and solve the crime. Unfortunately, nothing interesting like that seems to happen around Annie's neighborhood.

Marion Tickner

Nancy Drew Lives On

I received my first Nancy Drew book from my aunt whose favorite author was Joseph Lincoln. At the time Nancy was sixteen years old and drove her own car. No sixteen-year-old that I knew drove a car, much less had her own. But after all, this was a story and anything can happen in a story. We just let our imaginations run away with us.

During my years of reading about Nancy's adventures and misadventures, I never thought of looking for clues to solve the mystery before she did. I just let Nancy with Bess and George do the work.

One evening while watching a game show, possibly *What's My Line* or *To Tell The Truth*, the contestants claimed to be Carolyn Keene. What really surprised me was that the real writer of a Nancy Drew book was a man. How can that be? Carolyn is a girl's name. What I didn't know at the time was that some series, including Nancy Drew, were written by ghostwriters. In other words, different writers wrote some of the books under the byline Carolyn Keene.

When I started working, I haunted the secondhand bookstores to add to my collection. Eventually I married and moved away from home, packing my books in boxes to be stashed away in my attic. By then I had other favorite authors that I read when I had time.

The years passed, and the first thing I did after I retired was to clean out the attic. Out came the box of Nancy Drew Mysteries. On sunny summer afternoons I relaxed in the shade of a maple tree with a glass of iced tea and read those books again, one at a time. After reading the whole collection, I passed them on to my niece who had three young daughters.

Now that Nancy Drew has again come to my attention, I checked out two library books, thinking I had one old book and one new. One thing I noticed in the "old book" was that Nancy is no longer sixteen, and is now eighteen. The story was fast-moving, and I remembered the plot from when I'd read it years before. In the new book, written for younger readers, Nancy is eight years old.

I have since learned that some of the earlier books have been brought up to date for today's readers. In fact, some of the obsolete prose has been eliminated. Maybe that's the reason it seemed to be fast-moving, something I need to remember when writing for children. Now I wish I had my original copy of *Mystery of the Tolling Bell* to compare with the library book.

Nancy Drew lives on forever.

SARAH BROUSSARD WEAVER

An Open Letter to Nancy Drew

Dear Nancy,

I hope it's okay if I call you Nancy. I feel like I know you a little bit even though we've never officially spent any time together. I know it's my loss. You're such a legend, and I'm a little awed to even write you.

When I was a little girl, I played a lot with our mutual friends, the Hardy Boys and both sets of Bobbsey Twins. They talked about you sometimes. They said you were super fun and smart. I heard you were brave and solved all kinds of mysteries.

I wanted to get to know you. I met my other friends at thrift stores and garage sales, though, and I never saw you there. Maybe you were too good for those types of places. Maybe nobody who had you ever gave you up.

All I know is, I regret not meeting you when we were both young. It's kind of like how I regret not ever owning Girbaud jeans and not watching *Sex and the City* until it had been over for a few years.

Now I am middle-aged with kids, and I'm not sure we have much in common, Nancy. You're still so young and carefree, brave and strong. I'm in school full time, tired and grumpy. I don't even know how you never age like that. If it's due to your moisturizer, please let me know the name of it when you write back.

I don't have time to solve your kinds of mysteries because I'm busy solving *The Mystery of my Kid's Missing Shoe* and *The Mystery of the Stolen Reese's Peanut Butter Cup*. There's also *Who Hit Who First?* and *The Girl Who Hid Her Homework to Avoid Doing It.* Those are mysteries I deal with almost daily, and they would bore you. ➢

Nancy, I think I've already done the best thing I can do for our relationship. Seven years ago, I took my oldest daughter, a new reader, to the library and checked out some of the Nancy Drew Notebooks series for younger readers. Three years later, I took my next daughter, and last month I took my last daughter. When my son is old enough, I'll take him too. I don't know if he'll get along with the Hardy Boys better, though.

It's too late for us. I love you even though I've only held you in my arms briefly as I waited in the library checkout line. I love you for what you've done for us all, all the little reading girls everywhere.

SWAK,

Sarah Broussard Weaver

MERCEDES WEBB-PULLMAN

I longed to be you, Nancy Drew

Nancy Drew, Nancy Drew
I so admired you
for making sure that the Government's plans
stayed out of the spies' and agents' hands
and the double agents, too.

You had a boyfriend or two
Nancy Drew, Nancy Drew
but some had sinister thoughts in mind.
If his kiss was of the open-mouthed kind
you very quickly withdrew.

The Fascists, the Nazis too
were always after you
Nancy Drew, Nancy Drew. Each time you'd find
the clues and blueprints they left behind
but they still captured you.

You were so modern too
with radio in your shoe.
You always escaped, the cads subdued.
Your Mom and Dad couldn't know, Nancy Drew,
all that you'd been through.

The bravest spy was you
and the prettiest, too.
So sensitive, caring,
brave, bold and daring;
I longed to be you, Nancy Drew.

Lisa Wiley

Rereading Nancy Drew at 42

She's the It Girl—
an American classic like Grace Kelly

capable of becoming princess
of a glamorous coastal country.

With just a trace of lipstick,
and maybe a pair of pearl earrings,

she never resorts to sailor language,
always stands up for her best friends,

never leaves a man behind even if he's
dizzy from being clunked on the head

by a jewel thief. A little quirky,
she collects souvenir matchbooks,

stows an overnight bag in her car including
bathing suit for sleuthing in pleasant weather.

Raised by her housekeeper like Scout,
the kind of girl next door

I'd like my sons to meet
when the time is right—

resourceful, respectful, raincoat ready
to plug any leaking boat.

MARILYN ZELKE-WINDAU

Long Overdue

I'm reading Frank Dixon now.
It's a Hardy Boys Mystery.
I found it amongst your death's leavings.
The first page is mildewed.
It says, "After 30 days, return to Dave."

At bedtime, when I was eight,
I read Nancy's stories
of the moss-covered mansion
and the broken locket
and the old clock, attic, stagecoach.
I was in love with Ned Nickerson.

You were curled up in your own room,
on the daybed, with your heroes.

Night pulled shades down at 9 o'clock
but parental rules mustered youthful ploys.
A flashlight beamed bright my sheet shelter.
In your room a nightlight was the factor at play.

Batteried lights didn't burn holes in blankets.
They only woke us kids at 3.
Then, after droop-eyed bathroom calls,
our legs shifted mystery dog-eared pages
to bed bottom,
where reading would be resumed,
tented,
tomorrow.

Ksenya Makarova

Carson & Nancy

THE SECRET BOOKCASE

Sogol Shirazi

Nancy, Unmasked

JULIE E. BLOEMEKE

Triple Hoax

How I searched those promising titles,
their suggestive seductions: scarlet
slippers, brass-bound trunks, hollow
oaks that refused to reveal where.

How every mystery stopped me,
Ned and Nancy at another "No
Trespassing" sign, perfect set-up
of near lust again interrupted.

How could Ned and Nancy resist
all those heavy breathing phone calls,
that sensual slinking behind
moss-covered mansions, intense

whispers in the dim light of twisted
candles, the two of them, alone, crouched
under the hidden window, fingering
that spider sapphire in the dark?

Book after book, I began to get a clue,
suspect a double jinx, but still I held out,
determined to find the key

to Nancy's jewel box, the secret
of Shady Glen, hoping that Nancy
would rip off her velvet mask, slip

under the hidden staircase, unbutton
that old lace and say, here, Ned,
is the real twin dilemma.

But instead, there was only the persistent
mystery, the tease of the broken
locket, those damned leaning chimneys, ➤

the crossword cipher that kept me—
captive witness, dancing puppet—
from unveiling the silent suspect,

the true sinister omen, the phantom
trick behind the text,
the Carolyn Keene who wasn't

so Carolyn
or Keene,

who wrote Ned and Nancy
into perpetual chaste,
the hex of a wooden lady
who never held a secret after all.

Clue: 23 Nancy Drew titles below.

---

(1) The Triple Hoax (2) The Scarlet Slipper Mystery (3) The Mystery of the
Brass-Bound Trunk (4) The Message in the Hollow Oak (5) The Mystery at
the Moss-Covered Mansion (6) The Sign of the Twisted Candles (7) The
Hidden Window Mystery (8) The Spider Sapphire Mystery (9) The Double Jinx
Mystery (10) The Clue in the Jewel Box (11) The Secret of Shady Glen (12)
The Clue of the Velvet Mask (13) The Hidden Staircase (14) The Secret
in the Old Lace (15) The Twin Dilemma (16) The Clue of the Broken
Locket (17) The Clue of the Leaning Chimney (18) The Clue in the Crossword
Cipher (19) Captive Witness (20) The Clue of the Dancing Puppet (21) The
Silent Suspect (22) The Sinister Omen (23) The Secret of the Wooden Lady

TRICIA MARCELLA CIMERA

Nancy Herself

Years ago
in the dark ages, the early 1970s,
I lost a school library book.
I looked everywhere for it.
I retraced my steps,
reconstructed events,
deconstructed fruitless theories,
studied the facts carefully,
cast a narrowed eye on everyone,
just like a certain cool Girl Sleuth I loved.
I could *not* find that book—
checked out, never
to be checked back in.
Life was different back then for kids,
pre-millennial.
The School Librarian didn't
give me a gold star, an *atta-girl*,
for making a solid spunky effort to find it.
I had to replace it, *plus*
I was labeled a loser
for daring to lose it.
I finally had to tell
my parents about my crime;
they lectured me
on carelessness for days, weeks, months.
The book?
The new Nancy Drew
mystery that mysteriously
disappeared, never to be found again
despite my best attempts
to crack the case.

The irony only just came to me
when I wrote this poem
in celebration of
Nancy
herself.

Kathleen M. Heideman

Orange trees

Orange trees were burning everywhere

ELLEN COHEN

The Mystery of the Northern Lights is the last *Nancy Drew* novel of Carolyn Keene. The novel remained unfinished at the time of Keene's death, and the ending is unknown. The manuscript was recently discovered by Keene's great-grandniece in the author's old attic. It was written in an album and locked in a brass-bound trunk. The trunk went unnoticed for many years as it gathered dust near a leaning chimney. We have been granted permission to publish the first chapter that, we trust, will be greeted with delight by fans of the beloved detective.

The Mystery of the Northern Lights

Chapter 1

"Bess?"

Nancy Drew paused. It was not like the plucky, titian-haired girl to mull over her words. She took a breath as her friend, Bess Marvin, answered the phone. *How can I tell Bess about the latest mystery without frightening her?*

Nancy, eighteen, slender and attractive, was accustomed to being forthright. From the time she lost her mother at the age of three, she displayed self-confidence well beyond her years. A respected attorney in River Heights, her father, Carson Drew, often called upon Nancy to help with puzzling cases. Her courage and intelligence led her to solve mysteries that often eluded professional sleuths.

But today, the amateur detective fingered the buttons of her cardigan, a cornflower blue that matched the color of her eyes. The River Heights police captain, Chief McGinnis, had asked her to do him a personal favor. Nancy was fond of the genial captain. She had helped him on numerous occasions, and he, in turn, could be counted on when she found herself in perilous circumstances.

Just recently, for example, Chief McGinnis enlisted Nancy's help in *The Case of the Mistaken Bloodhound*. Nancy's keen instincts led her to a cave where a kidnapped photographer was being held after he unknowingly witnessed an art theft.

The photographer was hired for a fiftieth wedding anniversary at a moss-covered mansion. In the midst of the party, he happened to take a picture of the couple's scheming nephew as he carried a small, but valuable painting down the mansion's hidden staircase. Later, when the photographer disappeared, Chief McGinnis asked Nancy to intervene. Nancy was able to trace the photographer to the underground cave, outwitting a noted bloodhound that was also following the trail.

Now, Nancy was up against what would prove to be the most unusual mystery of her career. Chief McGinnis told her that a distant relative in Iceland had died, leaving no other heirs except himself. He had never met his great-aunt but heard she was eccentric. This aunt, Annabella, lived as a recluse on a farm in Iceland. The farm stood at the edge of the North Atlantic Ocean, against a backdrop of towering volcanoes. It was rumored that Annabella had amassed a great fortune by her association with a band of huge and hideous trolls who lived in the dark mountains and had a secret hoard of Viking treasure.

Chief McGinnis received a letter from an Icelandic solicitor, informing him of his aunt's death and mentioning the legacy that awaited him—on condition that he come to Iceland to claim it. The gift included a parcel of money, as well as several pieces of precious Viking silver. More perplexing, was that the exact whereabouts of the silver was not specified. The solicitor surmised that the trolls had confiscated it.

In the letter, it was noted that Great-aunt Annabella had left a series of cryptic clues, but these were only to be handed over in person, except for the first:

> *Search for the silver in the darkness of night.*
> *But beware–you may turn to stone at dawn's first light!*

"I have no idea what this means," Chief McGinnis told Nancy, shaking his head.

At present, the police chief was engaged in a delicate matter. A smuggling ring was operating in River Heights, run by a

120

group of cunning criminals that posed as Girl Scouts selling cookies. They used the empty boxes to transport jewels stolen from rich and unsuspecting elderly widows. Chief McGinnis was in the thick of the case and could not get away. He asked Nancy if she would travel to Iceland in his place.

"I trust you, Nancy. If anyone can decipher these clues, you can!"

The detective was flattered by the request, and told her father about it that evening at dinner. Carson Drew, a distinguished attorney, listened attentively to the story. The meal consisted of a delicious potato and leek soup, pork chops, and asparagus with Hollandaise sauce, prepared by Hannah Gruen. She had taken care of the Drew household since Nancy was a child. The housekeeper overheard the detective's conversation with her father. At the mention of "trolls," the kindly woman became alarmed.

"Oh, Nancy!" she said. "That sounds much too dangerous!"

But Carson Drew put down his fork and looked at his daughter. "Chief McGinnis has been a good friend to you," he said. "I think you should help him. I know the idea of trolls sounds farfetched, but you may be surprised to learn that the belief in trolls, and other such creatures, is widespread in Iceland."

"You're kidding, Dad!" said Nancy.

The lawyer continued. "I had a client from Reykjavik, the capital city of the country, who told me that although the people of Iceland are among the most educated in the world—ten percent of them have written books—over seventy percent believe in trolls! He himself was a sharp businessman with an international legal entanglement, but he too, held that belief."

"That seems highly improbable," said Nancy.

"I agree," said her father. "But one must retain a respect for other cultures and not let our own prejudices get in the way. Besides," he said, his eyes twinkling, "I'll bet you would enjoy a trip to Iceland. You can swim in the warm, mineral water of the Blue Lagoon and see the spectacular Northern Lights."

"I've heard about those lights," said Hannah Gruen, grudgingly. "They're supposed to be beautiful—pale green and pink lights in the night sky in northern countries like Sweden and Iceland. But I still think you shouldn't make the trip, Nancy. I don't believe in trolls, of course, but just in case . . ." Her voice trailed off. "Why, Nancy, you could get killed!"

Nancy stood up and put her arm around the housekeeper. "Don't worry, Hannah, dear," she said. "You know I'm always very careful."

"Why don't you see if your friends, Bess and George, can go with you," said Carson Drew. "I'm sure it would be much more fun to have them along."

"And safer, too," said Hannah Gruen, still with a look of concern on her face.

Bess Marvin and George Fayne were cousins, and two of Nancy's best friends. Bess was a pretty, slightly plump girl, with dimpled cheeks and soft blond hair. George, athletic and slim, had short dark hair and brown eyes.

While Bess's idea of a perfect afternoon was putting her feet up and indulging in a hot fudge sundae with whipped cream, George preferred long distance bike rides or white-water rafting. Though both girls had accompanied Nancy on many of her adventures, Bess shied away from anything with a hint of trouble, while George was always game for a fresh challenge.

"That's a great idea, Dad," said Nancy. "I think I'll call the girls and see if they're available."

"Let me know," said her father, "and I'll book your tickets. It's about a six-hour plane ride from here."

"I guess I'll have to leave my blue roadster behind," said Nancy, smiling. "It wouldn't be of any use crossing the ocean!"

"Make sure you bring plenty of warm clothes," said Hannah Gruen. "It can get very cold up there this time of year."

Nancy hugged the housekeeper. "How about helping me pack? That way you can make sure I have everything I need. And while I'm there, I'll buy one of those heavy sheep wool sweaters and bring you back a lovely wool scarf."

Hannah, still frowning, looked slightly appeased.

Nancy's pulse quickened. A trip to Iceland! She had never been to Scandinavia. With all those volcanoes, there was always the risk of a gigantic eruption! But she was excited to think about finding Annabella's treasure and giving Chief McGinnis his inheritance.

Nancy was sure George Fayne would be thrilled to accept her invitation. But she knew Bess, George's cousin, would waver. Though the idea of sampling pastries in a Scandinavian bakery would entice the girl, confronting a fearsome opponent, would not.

Nancy steeled herself as she dialed Bess's number.

She knew she had to warn her timid friend.

But how could she tell her? They might have to "lock horns" with treacherous trolls!

CHRISTINE COLLIER

Meeting Miss Drew

Nancy Drew, a cultural icon, is a fictional character in a mystery series that first appeared in 1930. The first four titles were an immediate hit. The books are ghostwritten by many authors under the collective pseudonym, Carolyn Keene, and first created by Edward Stratemeyer. The words clue, mystery, and secret are used the most often in the original titles. Some of the possible names considered for Nancy Drew were Stella Strong, Diana Dare, Nan Nelson, or Helen Hale. In France she is named Alice Roy, Kitty Drew in Sweden, Paula Drew in Finland, and in Germany, Susanne Langen. Macy's ordered six thousand copies of Nancy Drew books for the 1933 Christmas season, and sold out within days.

Before my love of Miss Marple, Agatha Raisin, and Harriet Vane, there was Nancy Drew. I first met Miss Drew in December 1959. That's a long time ago, and I was a student in the fifth grade. Our dedicated teacher gave each girl in our small class a Nancy Drew mystery book as a Christmas gift. This teacher was very practical and frugal and felt we would share our books with each other if we all got different titles. We did, and my love of the series began. My teacher signed and dated my book, *The Secret of the Wooden Lady,* and I have it still. It's the blue tweed version with endpapers showing other books in the series, an excellent sales promotion. On the outside of the cover is the silhouette of Nancy, bending slightly looking at the ground, and peering through a magnifying or quizzing glass. My friends and I immediately chose covers from the endpaper we hoped to read next. One coveted title was *The Ghost of Blackwood Hall.* After swapping books all winter, we were in mystery mode that spring; we felt there was something very strange about a large pile of brush and twigs behind the school. Certainly it moved each day, and positively did overnight. Was someone hiding in it and spying on them? We needed Nancy, our super sleuth.

In the summer of 1960, after school had ended for the year, my family was at a picnic at my Great-Aunt Flossie's house. She mentioned that her neighbor was having a rummage sale and we walked over to see what was available. In an old box of books I found a copy of *The Ghost of Blackwood Hall.* The asking price was one dime! I can still remember how excited I was when I asked my mother if I could get it and she readily agreed. I couldn't wait to tell my friends how I found it and that they were welcome to read another book in the series. It had a solid dark blue cover and the same silhouette. This end-paper had Nancy with magnifying glass, three women, a house, fence, and trees in a dark blue outline.

The second book in the series, *The Hidden Staircase,* is considered by many to be their favorite. My mother gave me other books, usually as gifts. A nearby family store named Danny Discount stocked children's books. For a special treat, we'd go there on shopping trips. Each child in my family got to buy something. My brother would get a Hardy Boys book and I'd get a new Nancy. I still remember trying to decide which one I'd choose out of the large selection.

Hoped-for expectations in Nancy Drew books are hidden doors, a haunted bridge or castle, moss-covered mansions, snake-infested ravines, locked trunks, statues with secret compartments, bookcases with moving shelves, mysterious wall panels, tunnels, caves, trap doors, spooky old attics, and passageways. You might find Nancy writing SOS messages backwards on whatever was available, preferably with a red lipstick on a windowpane or mirror, escaping from ropes, discovering hidden rooms under the stairs, or analyzing secret codes, strange handwriting, and suspicious footprints. Nancy is always prepared and carries a flashlight with extra batteries, a whistle, skeleton key, camera, candle, magnifying glass, and binoculars.

I am a freelance mystery writer and sure that reading Nancy Drew played a part in my writing style. My children's mystery, *Adventure on Apple Orchard Road,* tells the story of the Forrest family and the old house they buy. They find a letter from the past owner sharing that she and her husband have hidden things in the house for many years. Wonderful things like a time capsule, autographed Yankee baseball in the floor joists of the attic floor, an invisible ink pen stuffed inside an abandoned laundry chute in the pantry. Imagine how much fun it would be to live in a house like that. Another of my books, *Christmas at Cliffhanger Inn,* got the critical review, "Reads like a Nancy Drew." In other words, it was too simplistic for the reader. In my Christian romance, *A Heartfelt Christmas,* I have a hidden writing room under the staircase of another old house. Yes, I do have an old house, journal, and diary fetish. This room seems to be waiting for a future writer with an antique typewriter and comfy chair. Of course a journal is found, and it will divulge tidbits detailing important events about members of this household. I've always felt that reading personal letters or a diary in a book is the best form of guilty pleasure for revealing secrets. It's like snooping through a drawer or eavesdropping at a door.

Another Christmas my mother surprised me with a Dana Girls mystery book. I'd never heard of this collection. My mother said the author of Nancy Drew wrote it so she knew it would be good. The green tweed front cover had silhouettes of two young women and an expanded endpaper of this picture with an old house and a window with loose shutters, and broken railings on the steps. Later I received a Dana Girl cover in solid dark green with the same silhouette and endpaper. One woman is holding a flashlight with a light beam shining ahead and the other woman fearfully looking back. Loose shutters always spell danger! This detective series was about orphaned teenage sisters, Jean and Louise Dana, who solved mysteries while at their boarding school, Starhurst School for Girls. The books, less successful than the Nancy Drew series, were created in 1934 by the same publishers. It was an attempt to capitalize on Nancy Drew's popularity. Critics claimed that the sisters were "pallid followers in the dazzling train of Nancy Drew." However, I found reviews that stated some readers liked the mysteries better than Nancy Drew books, many finding them more mature. All Nancy Drew titles are listed above the Dana Girls titles, even in their own series, showing the preference of the publisher and that there was a direct connection between the two. Also, it served as a clever sales pitch for advertising everything written by the imaginary Carolyn Keene.

Mystery Guild offered a collection of Nancy Drew postcards picturing the classic dust jacket book covers, which are my personal favorites over the yellow "flashlight" editions. I lined the three-by-five-inch cards behind glass in a dark oak frame. It's a charming accent in my writing office. I'm very thankful I met Miss Drew of River Heights, America.

*Most of Nancy Drew lives in my garage except for the one
piece of her I keep near*

I boxed her up last spring, scanning her titles,
The Clue in the Diary, The Secret in the Old Attic,
fifty-somewhat books touching my hands.
My grandmother's basement smelt like must
covered in a decade of dirt. I wondered if
she ever came down and ran her hands along
my early childhood, most days spent at her house
while my parents worked factory and cleaning
jobs. I couldn't find her fingerprints, but plenty
of mildew collecting on the pages of *The Clue
in the Crumbling Wall.* I held the last book,
The Secret of the Golden Pavilion, in my hand,
and asked "What now, Nancy?" She looked
at me with magnifying glass clutched in hand,
and said, "There is no mystery here, Kristina.
Your grandmother is dead. It's too late to solve
anything. Shake off the cobwebs of the visits
you never made, the layers of unanswered
questions you never asked and move on."
I sneezed, closed the box, and leaned that
golden volume against my bookshelf at home.
It smells like dried raindrops cut into buttery
slices of toast my grandmother used to make.

DEIRDRE FLINT

The Ballad of River Heights

Some girls did theirs in neat order
with *The Secret of The Clock*,
Red Gate Farm was my first downfall
It was Nancy Drew nonstop.
Summer mornings, I'd awaken
Read straight through those balmy nights,
My world fell away and I was on a case in River Heights.
We did blackmail, theft and arson
I had a crush on your dad Carson

Nancy, Nancy Drew
I fell in deeper every clue
You got us out of every mess
You, me, George and Bess
And top-down in that car again
Your titian hair free in the wind
I was sitting next to you
The days that I slept, ate, breathed
Nancy Drew.

We chased crooks to England, Holland,
Istanbul, France and Peru.
You've been kidnapped, poisoned, drugged, shocked,
knocked unconscious, buried too.
Your dad let you flirt with danger,
confident you would survive.
And every time you wrecked your car
He had a new one in the drive.
No mom to ask you what you're doing
Just the kind old Hannah Gruen.

Nancy, Nancy Drew
Ned never laid a hand on you
With every case you won some more fans
Spinsters, invalids and orphans,
They all knew you'd nail your man
Oh, crime was so polite back then ➢

I was sitting next to you
The days that I slept, ate, breathed Nancy Drew.

One day they passed around Judy Blume
Forever and page 115
Nancy Drew seemed kind of trite
Way old-fashioned, too pristine
So farewell to that blue-eyed sleuth
The feisty hero of my youth
They've got a brand new series out,
Some say improved,
I can't see how . . .

Nancy, Nancy Drew
They went and they updated you
They took out each adverbial phrase
And Ned's not so hands-off these days
But top-down in that car again
Your titian hair free in the wind
I was sitting next to you
The days that I slept, ate, breathed Nancy Drew

Remember how you almost drowned
in *Mystery of The Tolling Bell?*
In *The Hidden Staircase*
You were knocked out when that ceiling fell?
Locked up in that castle
In The *Mystery of The Crumbling Wall*
Getting stuck in quicksand with Ned
In *The Ghost of Blackwood Hall*
Writing SOS upon the
Window of that speeding plane
Pigeons landing in your yard in
Password to Larkspur Lane
Trapped by your imposter in a
Submarine at Lilac Inn
Hanging out in Turkey in
The Mysterious Mannequin . . .

SHIVAPRIYA GANAPATHY

Tanka

1.

haunted bridge—
i saunter between
what is
and
what might be

2.

ticket trouble—
from under the rose bush
a hedgehog
watches
tonight's opera

3.

april fool's day—
i question my math
counting
crabs
on the seashore

mystery and madness

Day 1.

i search for secrets in old clocks and hidden staircases. i long for a lilac-scented mystery.

Day 6 .

i am hidden in shadow, don't try to find me. i'm locked behind a red gate. i keep secret diaries, send encrypted letters to strangers.

Day 9.

i've learned to eat by the light of twisted candles, underneath an old sign marked larkspur lane. i dream of broken lockets hidden in hollow oaks, with ivory charms standing watch while whispering statues tell tales of haunted bridges. every day, there are phantom sounds of tapping heels sending clues. asking am i the mystery, or are you?

Day 14.

i sit on a brass-bound trunk inside a moss-covered mansion, unfolding a neatly folded missing map found in a jewel box.

Day 27.

i spend rainy saturdays in old attics, looking at crumbling walls and singing made-up songs to tolling bells, leafing through a stack of old albums. i remember that winter in an inn called blackwood hall, with the leaning chimney and a toy wooden lady balanced on the very edge of the front desk. we walked all the way to the ski jump and imagined what it would be like to speed down the mountain with nothing more than a velvet mask, a secret, and a scarlet slipper.

Day 45

instead of sleep, i make notes under the shade of witch trees, searching for you in hidden windows. you are hard to find. i am easy to find. i'm always right here, wearing a charm bracelet with tiny black keys and a silver showboat.

Day 60

i'm here and i'm going mad, dreaming of a golden pavilion which never existed and an old stagecoach that did. she is your fire dragon and i am a dancing puppet, living in a moonstone castle, my lullabies the sound of whistling bagpipes. i tell you i am on pine hill, and she tells you she is exactly 99 steps from you. I am a cipher who longs to be a spider sapphire, and you are an invisible intruder within my mystery.

Day 93

i want to be as mysterious as a mannequin, but end up with a crooked banister for a spine and a mirror for a face. look at me, and i will jinx you with my glowing eyes and promises of forgotten cities. i don't want to be a phantom anymore, i write in a strange message to halley's comet. i have no more questions to devour: my crocodile appetite subsides, allows a pearl to grow in my stomach.

Day 100

the

Titles Found in "Mystery and Madness"

The Secret of the Old Clock
The Hidden Staircase
The Bungalow Mystery
The Mystery at Lilac Inn
The Secret at Shadow Ranch
The Secret of Red Gate Farm
The Clue in the Diary
Nancy's Mysterious Letter
The Sign of the Twisted Candles
The Password to Larkspur Lane
The Clue of the Broken Locket
The Message in the Hollow Oak
The Mystery of the Ivory Charm
The Whispering Statue
The Haunted Bridge
The Clue of the Tapping Heels
The Mystery of the Brass-Bound Trunk
The Mystery at the Moss-Covered Mansion
The Quest of the Missing Map
The Clue in the Jewel Box
The Secret in the Old Attic
The Clue in the Crumbling Wall
The Mystery of the Tolling Bell
The Clue in the Old Album
The Ghost of Blackwood Hall
The Clue of the Leaning Chimney
The Secret of the Wooden Lady
The Mystery at the Ski Jump

The Clue of the Velvet Mask
The Ringmaster's Secret
The Scarlet Slipper Mystery
The Witch Tree Symbol
The Hidden Window Mystery
The Clue of the Black Keys
The Haunted Showboat
The Secret of the Golden Pavilion
The Clue in the Old Stagecoach
The Mystery of the Fire Dragon
The Clue of the Dancing Puppet
The Moonstone Castle Mystery
The Clue of the Whistling Bagpipes
The Phantom of Pine Hill
The Mystery of the 99 Steps
The Clue in the Crossword Cipher
The Spider Sapphire Mystery
The Invisible Intruder
The Mysterious Mannequin
The Crooked Banister
The Secret of Mirror Bay
The Double Jinx Mystery
Mystery of the Glowing Eye
The Secret of the Forgotten City
The Sky Phantom
The Strange Message in the Parchment
Mystery of Crocodile Island
The Thirteenth Pearl

TRICIA KNOLL

The Secret at Shadow Ranch
                —the fifth Nancy Drew volume

Oh give me a home

where shadows share
mirror limbs and leanings

whisper, weighing
nothing, casting backwards.

In slipshod light, gallop me
somewhere new.

When shadows evaporate
at corners, play hide and seek.

When they beg to race,
saddle up. Stow your secret

watch, find the red-rock cave,
listen to the old woman's wisdom.

Stretch me longer
than before.

Sedoka for The Secret of the Old Clock

An aristocrat,
Drew dislikes the Topham snobs
And discredits their sisters.

She obtains the Clock,
The clue to the deceased's will,
And the money from Topham.

Etheree for The Clue of the Velvet Mask

Drew
hinders
the act of
stealing artworks.
A black velvet hood
is the clue between masks
having certain dates displayed
on which some robberies took place.
She finds out why Peter Tombar owns
some properties and what secrets he hides.

Tyburn for The Clue of the Tapping Heels

Smitten,
Hidden,
Carter's,
Kittens!
Fred has smitten you to hide the funds!
Drew twigged that Fred trapped Carter's kittens.

JAMES PENHA

A Cento to Nancy Drew
    from the sixty-four titles of her books published by
    Grosset & Dunlap from 1930 to 1981

Remove that velvet mask
your eyes glowing with cold
and the twin dilemma—
double jinx—of wind
whistling like bagpipes
that carries you invisible
intruder down
from the ski jump
on Pine Hill (where
until the thirteenth pearl
you were a sky phantom,
a witness captive
to the mystery of the fire dragon
on Crocodile Island
far below in the middle of Mirror Bay)
to find along Larkspur Lane
the red gate
in the crumbling wall
between the whispering statue
and the hollow oak
—the witch tree—
of a shadow ranch
and like a mannequin
or puppet
dance across
the haunted bridge
on which the ghost
who reigned once as the wooden lady
of the moss-covered mansion
with its golden pavilion
will point her finger
bejeweled with the ring
of the swami who damned her ➢

to a moonstone saucer flying
far beyond the bungalow
of Lilac Inn
above a forgotten city
where you shall ride
in an old stagecoach
to Blackwood Hall
before a hidden window broken
but unlocked with the black key
on the ring round
the kachina in your pocket
so that you shall find
a staircase hidden
behind an old grandfather clock
in what seemed a leaning chimney
and follow its crooked banister
tapping your heels
upon each of the 99 steps
to an old attic where
atop a brass-bound trunk
covered in old lace
in diary pages pasted
in an old album
in a jewel box
lined with a scarlet slipper
beneath a triple hoax
of ivory candles
twisted and charmed
to represent a Greek symbol
a mysterious letter
with a strange message in its parchment
a crossword cipher?
or the missing map!
to find the spider sapphire.

Patrick T. Reardon

The Birth of Nancy Drew

She is an attractive girl of eighteen,
driving a new, dark-blue convertible,
a birthday present.
She is blond and blue-eyed,
and she helps her father
with his puzzling law cases.

"My intuition."

Five-year-old Judy
darts into the road,
narrowly avoids a van,
climbs a wall
and falls.

"Oh, my goodness."

She slams on brakes
and finds Judy
at the foot of the embankment,
half in the river water.
She lifts the girl
and carries her to the house by the road.

"I'm sure she'll be alright."

Judy and two great-aunts,
forgotten in Josiah Crowley's will
and—they now discover—victimized
by shady men stealing silver,
both short and heavyset,
one with dark hair, one with light,
both with large noses,
driving the van that
nearly killed Judy!

"I'll try to catch the van!"

KATHLEEN M. HEIDEMAN

I can't imagine what

Nancy Reddy

The Case of the Double Jinx

THE SCARLET SLIPPER MYSTERY
You're Nancy Drew and you drive a blue coupé.
You drive fast. Your mother is dead.
She's the new-hired help and you're a nosy houseguest.
She's a model turned jewel thief and you're hot
on her trail. She's a pretender to the fortune
of the county's richest missing bachelor.
You're solving mysteries that stump the cops.
You sass them back. You're flip-haired and eagle-eyed.
You're a daredevil detective on the trail of a breathtaking
escape. She fooled you once and won't again.

THE FOOTPRINTS IN THE FLOWERBEDS
You're peering in her windows. You're watching
as she hides the proof beneath the sink,
as she scrubs her hands with lye. She splashes bleach
across the tile. You're watching as she runs
the bath. You watch. She's wasp-waisted
and flaxen-haired. You're not the better sister.
You're no one's good-time gal. You're a bayou,
a river caught fire. You're armed with flashlight
and revolver. You're casing the estate.
Ned will get you for your date at four. He's late.

THE MYSTERY OF THE WOODEN LADY
She's a cocktail dress and you're day-old rye.
You find a blond hair on the sofa bed,
stockings in the spare room. You come home late
one night and find your house lit like a birthday.
You tiptoe to the window, your skirt's hem
catching on the hedges. She's in your house.
She's dancing slow with fickle Ned. She laughs
at all his jokes. Now you're a pincushion.
You're the sulfur smell of rotten eggs. You do
the only thing you can. You run. ➤

THE CLUE IN THE BREAKFAST NOOK
You run home to River Heights. You bolt the door.
You're a sure shot, an expert swimmer,
a gourmet cook. You bake birthday cakes
and ice them all with arsenic. You learn to knit.
You believe in the jinx. You won't say his name,
won't look at the phone. She's a damsel
in dishwashing gloves. She's at your kitchen table,
sugaring her tea. Ned's a lost sock.
She smiles your smile and wears his jacket.
She hums. You're gimlet-eyed. You're losing steam.

THE SECRET LOST AT SEA
This time you're the belle of Miami Beach.
You're busting up a gang of smugglers.
You drink rum and dance all night. You learn
to surf. A strange man licks the saltwater
from your hair. The smugglers are setting sail
for Cuba. You're an inside job. You're on their tail.
There's a girl here dressed as you. You surprise her
on the ship's back stairs. Now the jig is up.
You're found out, tied up, left to drown.
You tap dance SOS against the cabin's roof.

.

THE CASE OF THE DISAPPEARING HUSBANDS
You're on vacation in the snow-stunned Alps
when the innkeeper comes to you for help.
He's getting threats from a dark-wigged woman
who claims that she's your twin. You're snowed in.
He tells you all the town's most handsome men
go missing after dark. You wear a borrowed mink
and sleuth by candlelight. You smell Ned's soap.
She's a false wall. She's a trap door. You're dangling
from the rafters. Ned's tied up in the basement.
He's bound and gagged. He's never been so grateful.

THE STRANGE MESSAGE ON THE TRAILHEAD
You get him back but he won't stay.
Silly Ned, he wanders off. He's lost
in state parks, disappears on dinner dates.
You're on the case. He's lucky. You rescue him,
time and time again. You get him back
in pieces. You swear you hear his voice
before the dial tone clicks on. You find
his toenail clippings on the tile. His name's
a rock you rub against your teeth.
He's a wishbone saved beside the kitchen sink.

THE INVISIBLE INTRUDER
You're digging through her trashcan. You're watching
as she slips the proof beneath her skin.
Her body now the briefcase full of unmarked bills.
She scrapes her palms against the wall's fresh paint.
She swings a bag of bones into the yard.
Her hands flush red and you know you'll never
see that boy again. Born different
you could have been sisters. Like those butterflies
in shadowboxes, pinned and mounted above the mantle.
Now you're the double agent. You're calling all the shots.

THE GIRL WHO COULDN'T REMEMBER
You're creeping through her flowerbeds.
There's no crime to detect here but your own
and Ned's long gone. You're the back door's loose latch,
the spare key beneath the mat. You're pawing
through her dresses, pirouetting in her heels.
She's in your town now. You're in her hair.
One quick slit and you're in the space inside
her skin. You hold your breath then whisper.
You thumb the ligaments. You kick the tires.
You loved that dumb boy, too. Before he died. ➢

THE TRIPLE HOAX

She's a foxtrot. She's a jinx and you can't speak.
You're a dahlia and she's the state fair's
bright-eyed Susans. Or she's the real Nancy
and you're a costume party. Didn't you feel
made of paper? Didn't you hide for years
from houses, the streets of windows
that left you feeling skinned and eyed? Even
the neighbor's house for sale, the mulch and rows
of transplant tulips, their faces open—
how their black stamens stared and stripped you bare.

Massimo Soranzio

Time for Mystery, Nancy Drew!

Wooden lady, mysterious mannequin,
Kachina doll, whispering statue,
Invisible intruder from a forgotten city,

Sky phantom, captive witness
To mystery and secrets,
Double jinx, triple hoax or twin dilemma:

A glowing eye behind a velvet mask,
The tapping heels of a dancing puppet's
Scarlet slipper—99 steps to the old attic . . .

What shadow ranch or moss-covered mansion
Will your quest lead you to this time,
On Pine Hill, on Crocodile Island, or at Mirror Bay?

Will you take an old stagecoach,
Board a haunted showboat or a flying saucer,
Or ski jump, following a Fire Dragon?

What will an old album reveal, or a secret diary?
Look out for a hidden window or staircase,
Mind the crooked banister, the crumbling wall . . .

Where will you find your next clue—
By the witch tree, or in the hollow oak?
In a jewel box, or in a brass-bound trunk?

Greek symbol or crossword cypher?
A mysterious parchment or a missing map?
Whistling bagpipes or a tolling bell?

And what about that spider sapphire,
The Swami's ring, or the thirteenth pearl?
The old clock is ticking: time for mystery!

LEA SHANGRAW FOX

No Good Stumpy Dowd

VIRGINIA CHASE SUTTON

The Bungalow Mystery
 —published 1930

Even at the start of a series, only the third book in,
it is clear there will be solved mysteries and happy
endings all around. But to begin, Nancy and her pal
Helen Corning go boating on a lovely day at camp and

end up nearly drowned. Laura, a frail but plucky young
orphaned heiress, saves their lives and Nancy's quivering
nose for mysteries sends her on escapades, all
designed to fit irregular puzzle pieces together. The

novel involves male look-alikes, Nancy slammed
on the head by a gun's muzzle, a stolen inheritance,
a wish for Carson Drew's revolver, threats to report
Nancy to the cops for being nosy, breaking and

entering a couple of times, wild car rides on dirt
highways that are either just rolled or deeply rutted.
Nancy worms her way into the mysteries all by
herself, no help from Helen, who is just a walk-on,

not much help from Laura, who needs Nancy the most.
O, there is a chained man in a damp dungeon, Nancy
tied with a heavy rope and left to die, along with the man,
Laura's true guardian. Fortunately, she knows how to untie

the bonds, thanks to a demonstration she viewed recently by
a detective. She holds her arms just so and they manage to
escape. Stolen inheritance on the line, Carson Drew loads that
revolver, shoves it in a pocket, takes the young heiress on

a hair-raising car ride, as they chase her guardian's imposter,
the scoundrel Stumpy Dowd. Bullets fly, missing Carson
and the girls, who travel behind his practical sedan in Nancy's
blue roadster. But Stumpy has a crack-up and nearly

dies in the accident. His sports car—purchased with
some of Laura's money—bursts into flames and Nancy
bravely pulls out two suitcases, one of which contains ➣

Laura's money and her guardian's as well. Then the

vehicle explodes, raining car parts. Stumpy is rushed
to the hospital and will be jailed for thirty years, Carson
predicts. Laura is united with the correct guardian, her
fortune of one-hundred-thousand dollars safe, making

her a wealthy young lady, set for life. She rewards Nancy, who
protests, finally agrees to accept an expensive jeweled necklace
as she collects souvenirs from each of her mysteries. At the novel's
conclusion, it predicts Nancy's adventuring days are not over. Soon

she will be off on another quest after spending the summer with her
gal pals knowing the love of mysteries would always be with her. The
audience, hooked on Nancy's gold hair, brains, pluck and luck, want
the next novel and those to follow, with Nancy as heroine, girl detective.

MELANIE VILLINES

Sally Draper reads The Clue of the Black Keys

In Season 4, Episode 9 of *Mad Men,* "The Beautiful Girls," ten-year-old Sally Draper hops a commuter train and moves between cars to avoid the conductor because she has no money for the fare. It's 1964. People are protesting the Vietnam War and picketing for Civil Rights. Sally, too, is protesting her life—especially her parents' divorce. She's running away from mean mom Betty in the suburbs to fun dad Don in the city. An older woman rescues Sally and brings her to the Madison Avenue ad agency where Don Draper is creative director. Sally stays overnight at her father's Greenwich Village apartment, and the next afternoon she's in Don's office reading *The Clue of the Black Keys,* Nancy Drew Mystery #28—a book that deals with archaeological digs in Mexico and stolen cultural artifacts, with the villains a married couple posing as scientists. Is it a coincidence that Sally is vying with her parents and the book's dastardly duo is a husband and wife? Did Sally bring the book with her from Ossining? Did she have it at her dad's apartment or office? Did a secretary run out and buy it to keep her occupied? She's halfway through the book, so she probably brought it from home. When Sally ran away, she couldn't leave it behind because she was eager to find out what happened. In the book's opening chapter, "An Urgent Request," on the first page, Nancy says to Bess, "Wasn't it a grand weekend in New York?" Perhaps Sally likes reading about a girl who visits Manhattan, a girl with no mother, no one to tell her what to do and who to hang out with and what to wear and how to feel and how to behave or when she can cut her hair. Sally believes her Ossining home is haunted with her grandfather's ghost. Her kind nanny Carla has disappeared. And her brother Bobby keeps shape shifting—played by three different actors in four seasons. Then there's the mystery of her father, who is not really Don Draper at all, but a man on the lam named Dick Whitman. As Sally pores over her Nancy Drew book, Don walks into his office and tells his daughter that her mother will arrive in five minutes to pick her up. Sally proclaims, "I'm not going back! I hate it there!" When her father insists, Sally tries to run away again, leaving Nancy Drew open on the chair. After falling on her face while trying to flee, Sally is forced to leave with Betty—with no time to retrieve her book. Did she ever learn how the story turned out? Did she ever read another Nancy Drew mystery? Or did this experience propel her into darker material?

Nancy Drew's Conundrum

The secret of the old clock was stashed in
The hidden staircase under
The crooked banister, but
The clue in the diary alluded to
The sign of the twisted candles.
The invisible intruder had disembarked
The haunted showboat to look for
The clue in the old stagecoach, just as
The mysterious mannequin and
The phantom of Pine Hill found
The clue in the old album, at the foot of
The haunted bridge.
The whispering statue supposed
The message in the hollow oak was
The Ring Master's secret, he was a
Captive witness of
The twin dilemma and
The strange message in the parchment was
The Greek symbol in
Nancy's mysterious letter.
The thirteenth pearl had been hidden in
The Swami's ring which led
The sky phantom to assume it was
The triple hoax, but he later discovered
The clue in the jewel box was
The password to Larkspur Lane.

HIDDEN TREASURES
(Found & Erasure Poems)

             an attractive girl   was

         convertible
some
         sweet   car for
                            fun
   his work
                         a well-known
                      River
                      of

   Smiling
     intuition

                      in horror
                         a   girl

                                     was
   barely   her

E. KRISTIN ANDERSON

an attractive girl

an attractive girl was
convertible
some
sweet car for
fun
his work
a well-known
River
of
Smiling
intuition
in horror
a girl
was
barely her

LEA SHANGRAW FOX

You've Been Poisoned

STEVE BOGDANIEC

Captions Drew Chapter Titles Nancy

"Nancy has been poisoned!" the doctor announced
alarm hints fails the detective
puzzling paper treachery

"How strange!" Hannah murmured
fantastic double headlines
stolen story tactics
dog gift missing

George and Bess rushed forward to help Nancy
phantom sleuths
missing the dream

"Hang on, Nancy!" Tex shouted
sheriff's nettle ride
startling red warning schoolmaster king

Could she trap the thief in this disguise? Nancy wondered
end revelation hoax
the lawsuit entrance

"At least I have a sketch of the intruder's footprints," Nancy
said to herself
steps to the cliff's strange scare
sudden parchment disappearance

"I must get out of here!" Nancy thought desperately
the dangerous sneak
exciting triple gift double prowler

Suddenly Nancy spotted the mysterious Arab
the desperado's sinister red lights
curious secret suspect

"We must find the other part of the paper," Nancy said ➤

detective Nancy's clue
the dog gift missing

"Never try to pierce the gypsies' secrets, or misfortune will
befall you!" the woman whispered
fortuneteller's helpful news
danger treasure of perilous quest
foiled ghosts

"Come and rope me, pardner!" Bud challenged Bess
rewarding Nancy's artist: a doll
shortcut rockslide

"What are you doing?" George called to the stranger
backstage surprises lion armor
complications interrupted source dismissal
investigates shadow property

"Drop that purse!" Nancy cried out
upsetting reunion of Warwick, the daring financier
prisoner stolen valuable program
curious footprints

"Get that blanket out of this house!" Hannah cried
interrupted knight followed gold
strange victories

"I won't go there! It's haunted!" Trixie called out
in shorty's haunted frightened blue clue
the mannequin's present impostor

The shock knocked them into the flower bed
amazing rattle attack
strange light purse

"I am being followed!" Nancy thought anxiously
two stranger trick
dream the strategy

156

"Halt! Or I'll run you through!" the knight cried out
warning Nancy
green figure escaped tracing in dancing

"It's one of Mrs. Struthers' stolen dolls!" Nancy exclaimed
bride disguise
house hidden television revelation
unexpected tack clue

"Leave here at once and never come back!" the stranger
warned
search the collector
room assignment
dungeon without program

"Nancy, be careful!" Bess cried fearfully
warning from gold stranger
number nine clue surprising confession

ESCAPE

connected with

mystery

open

to

wait   and

see

watch

puzzle   over

appearance

see-

ing

the phantom

return

again.

Escape

connected with

mystery

open

to

wait and

see

watch

puzzle over

appearance

see-

ing

the phantom

return

again.

Mathias Jansson

Create Your Own Nancy Drew Mystery Story

The	Secret	of the	Old	Clock
	Hidden	at	Red	Staircase
	Sign	in	Shadow	Mystery
	Mystery		Twisted	Inn
	Haunted		Broken	Ranch
	Clue		Hollow	Farm
	Quest		Black	Letter
	Phantom		Velvet	Diary
	Mysterious		Golden	Candles
	Ghost		Dancing	Lane
	Password		Whistling	Oak
	Message		Ivory	Statue
	Invisible		Whispering	Charm
			Tapping	Locket
			Missing	Keys
			Crumbling	Jump
			Leaning	Mask
			Dancing	Secret
			Crooked	Symbol
			Glowing	Showboat
				Statue
				Bridge
				Map
				Hill
				Album
				Box
				Bell
				Chimney
				Attic
				Lady
				Pavilion
				Bagpipes
				Stagecoach
				Mannequin

Trapdoors

down the corridor
like a secret tunnel
a sleuth cautions silence
when all the words are foreign
or perhaps criminal—those
possibly being watched
by the old milkman
faint at first sight
of barbecue

"Do you know ▆▆▆
they ▆▆▆ '
▆▆▆ wore masks.''
'▆▆▆'' ▆▆▆ trying to hide
▆ rising excitement.
▆▆▆▆▆▆
▆▆▆▆▆▆''▆
▆▆▆▆shame▆▆▆ ▆
▆▆'
▆▆▆▆ no heed to the words. ▆▆
▆▆▆▆''▆▆▆
'▆▆ a peculiar mark on the ▆▆▆
▆▆▆' ▆▆▆
▆▆▆ "▆▆▆
▆▆ child.
▆▆▆▆ ▆▆▆'
▆▆▆▆ a means of iden-
tifying ▆▆▆ ▆▆▆
life story is ▆ fantastic ▆▆▆ speak
▆ it.''
▆▆▆ ▆▆▆ ▆▆▆
▆▆▆ ▆▆▆
and help ▆▆▆.
The young ▆▆▆ rise ▆▆▆
▆▆▆
▆▆▆ try to move,'' ▆▆▆ kindly.
▆▆ take ▆▆▆ ▆▆▆ ▆▆▆
up your guard, ▆▆ then they can carry you ▆
▆▆▆
lifted ▆▆▆ ▆▆▆ ▆▆▆

KAREN MASSEY

Do You Know They Wore Masks?

Do you know they wore masks,
trying to hide rising
excitement, shame;
no heed to the words,
a peculiar mark on the child,
a means of identifying

Life story is fantastic:
speak it,
and help the young rise
Try to move kindly,
take up your guard,
then they can carry you,
        lifted

The Mystery at Lilac Inn

The Mystery at Lilac Inn
Nancy Drew number four
interpreted by Mark Hudson
4/6/2018

SARAH NICHOLS

An Encounter

Another mystery has me.
She comes out of a
long silence

warning me of
a
secret unraveling.

A little body.
A cry.

My bitter reward
for knowing

everything.

M.A. Scott

An Amazing Revelation

She   tried
     to fix you

     to finish the meaning

She   was practicing
     flew away inside, blazing
     white as laryngitis

She   was the dancing puppet
          with hardly any voice left

     one night
     diamonds   pearls   rubies   stones
     stared at her
     causing her light to shine

She   rose,
          white as melted aluminum

     smiled and shook her head

          I'm ready for a new mystery

SHLOKA SHANKAR

Interior Monologue

Come back for more.
Act mysterious, sound obnoxious.
Cry in private
like a well-meant warning.
Tell me about some
thing you lost decked in
red and green bows.
Keep your head while
walking up a slippery roof.
Be aware. Riddle and fortune
won't mix tonight.

A. GARNETT WEISS

With original mystery

Secret shadow
   in the diary letter

     sign, password, broken
     the message, hollow, whispering
     the missing clue

     jewel black velvet slipper
     symbol of the golden dragon
     dancing phantom steps
     in the crooked mirror

     the jinx, the glowing eye
     forgotten
     the sky—parchment, island pearl

hidden 60 years

LORETTE C. LUZAJIC

Carson's Angels

THE CASE OF CAROLYN KEENE

KAITLYNN NICHOL

Nancy Drew Silhouette

SYLVIA CAVANAUGH

Mildred Wirt
  Lipogram after Mark Zimmerman

Riddle
Will
will it
tell
Time
limit

Drew tried
Drew ID'd Mr.s
Drew wielded
        wire
Drew Did!

Wirt, Write!

Photo from Jennifer Fisher's collection showing Mildred Wirt Benson in the 1980s holding her first ghostwritten Nancy Drew book, *The Secret of the Old Clock* (New York: Grosset & Dunlap, 1930).

JENNIFER FISHER

Mildred Wirt Benson—The Real Nancy Drew, Biography

NANCY & ME

Like many Nancy Drew fans, there was just something about Nancy that kept me turning the pages! My zeal for mysteries and Nancy's smart capable adventuresome self were a match made in literary heaven. I devoured the books in the late 1970s through the 1980s, when Nancy Drew classic hardcovers spun off into paperbacks and other series like the more modern Nancy Drew Files. There were plenty of Nancy Drew books to satisfy me. Between visits to the bookstore and my school library, I was beginning on a journey that even then I had no clue I would be embarking on.

Within a decade of leaving my childhood books safely ensconced at my parent's home and taking off for college and law school, I would never have predicted that I'd end up rediscovering Nancy Drew and beginning a massive collection of all things Drew. Soon after the collecting bug set in, I began heading up a group of wonderful Nancy Drew fans, Nancy Drew Sleuths. Soon after came consulting with licensee companies creating Nancy Drew products, working at times with the publishers of Nancy Drew on books and merchandise, consulting on the 2007 Nancy Drew Warner Brothers movie, writing a book, *Clues for Real Life: The Classic Wit & Wisdom of Nancy Drew* for a licensee, and licensing Nancy Drew for our own line of merchandise. I've been interviewed on the *Today Show* and other media outlets. I plan our annual Nancy Drew Conventions and other gatherings. Really, it never ends and it's been a wonderful diversion from a planned legal career.

When I first got on the Internet around 1997, there was an old, now-defunct, message board by publisher Applewood Books for Nancy Drew fans. I met other collectors and fans and started to learn more about Nancy Drew. I'd found a vintage 1930s version of *The Hidden Staircase* at an antique mall and had become very intrigued at the difference between it and my childhood early-80s version, a yellow hardcover with a much shorter story inside. Then there was eBay and now, nearly twenty years later, I have added to my childhood books to amass around four thousand books, collectibles, art, and other paper ephemera.

THE LEGEND OF CAROLYN KEENE

For as much fun as I've had delving into all things Nancy Drew, something even more amazing happened. I got to meet Carolyn Keene. *The* Carolyn Keene. The original, Mildred A. Wirt Benson, who wrote *The Secret of the Old Clock* at age twenty-four in 1929. It was published, along with the next two books in the series, on April 28, 1930.

Growing up and reading these books, you picture Nancy Drew in various ways—often based on the book illustrations. You don't conjure up a picture of Carolyn Keene as easily. It's really easy to ponder the question of who Carolyn Keene is and what motivates her. Is she a magnet for mysteries, where does she get all her story ideas, and is she some sort of detective when she's not hammering out new mystery stories? These are just a few of the questions that fans young and old alike routinely ask me. If these books were first written in the 1930s, then who is still writing them today, over eighty-five years later? The secret has been out for some time, but Carolyn Keene was a pen name for ghostwriters who have written these books and various spinoffs and continue to do so on the currently published series. The classic series familiar to most people—books 1-56—had eight ghostwriters.

When I joined that online message board, I began hearing things about a woman living in Toledo, Ohio, working at the *Toledo Blade*, who wrote the first Nancy Drew books. Millie was in her nineties and still working, with no plans for retirement. I was amazed. And intrigued. Who dreams they'll get to meet a real Carolyn Keene—especially the original?

176

MEETING "CAROLYN KEENE"

It was a spectacularly promising night on April 10, 2000, when another collector and I formed a discussion group online for Nancy Drew fans, calling it "Nancy Drew Sleuths" (NDS). We discussed books and collected and traded books. One of our members lived in Toledo, and he had met Millie several times and had books signed by her. He encouraged me to come visit Millie. I suggested a trip to my mom and explained the somewhat urgent matter—after all, Millie was ninety-five and as much as she never wanted to exit this world, time was of the essence, more than I realized.

Later that year, our NDS group put together a scrapbook for Millie and expressed our appreciation of her writing and our love of Nancy Drew, and we presented it to her through our local member during the holidays. She later wrote of it in "Basement Work One for the Books." In the article, she wrote about finding an old ledger—where she'd recorded every story and book she'd written—which she gave to another collector for safekeeping "to be preserved as valuable memorabilia." In its place was our scrapbook, and she noted, "Replacing the space vacated in my collection is artwork presented to me as an honorary member of the Sleuths, an organization of Nancy Drew fans. This material, though only recently created, is more interesting than any old record book, but it will undoubtedly become more valuable with each passing year." Over a decade later, in December 2013, I would bid on this same scrapbook when the estate of Millie's daughter Peggy was auctioned off. I won the auction and retrieved the scrapbook and *Honorary Sleuth Award* we presented to Millie after our Toledo gathering during the summer of 2001.

In 2001, my mom and I made plans for a fun spring road trip from Texas to Ohio, and we book hunted and antiqued our way to Ohio, where eleven other members of the group met as part of our first unofficial, at the time, convention. One day, I met Millie at the *Toledo Blade* where she was working, and she interviewed me for her article about our group's visit, "Nancy

Drew Sleuths Follow Trail to Author of Books." I also interviewed her for an article I was writing for a series zine, and she signed some of my books—including my first edition of *The Secret of the Old Clock* from 1930. It was such a surreal experience to sit down and chat with her. She was very intelligent and seemed genuinely interested in learning more about the group and what we did. By this point in her life, after she was revealed as Carolyn Keene at the 1993 Nancy Drew Conference, a lot of traffic came her way from fans and revelers—which often interrupted her work days. Most of the time, she took it in stride, even if she didn't sometimes understand what all the fuss was about. She was great about meeting with our group and signing our books the next day.

While interviewing me for her article, she was rather intrigued about our discussion group and expressed consternation over my title as the discussion group's "moderator"—she didn't like it for her article, so she decided to appoint me president of the group, and the rest was history . . .

MILLIE & ME

After our first meeting, I spoke with her occasionally on the phone to check in. I was writing a couple of articles about her and Nancy Drew and also something on her favorite Penny Parker Mystery Stories. I sometimes just wanted to touch base with her and usually had a few questions. Sometimes she'd ask for story ideas for her column. There were some things she didn't want to talk about—like her involvement with the 1980 trial between the Nancy Drew publishers. There was also advice for me. I'd gone to law school to be a lawyer, but I had always loved writing and dabbled in that throughout my life. After graduating law school, I went in another direction with the NDS group and the consulting. One day she said to me, "Maybe you'll become a writer instead of working as a lawyer," and she seemed to encourage it. That was inspiring, and it has led to numerous articles and op-eds, as well as where I am today, writing her biography.

After having such a wonderful time in Toledo, members of the group decided we should do this yearly. So we planned a

178

second convention for spring 2002 in Iowa City, Iowa, where the 1993 Nancy Drew Conference had taken place, and a visit to Millie's childhood home in Ladora, Iowa. Millie was interested in our planned visit to her childhood home and wrote about it in her column, "Nancy Drew Fans Search for the Details." Early 2002 had brought her retirement—something she fought off and on for years—but it was a working retirement, for she was still coming in to write a monthly column. During the first few months of the year, the media—NBC, CNN, and others—regularly paraded through the newsroom filming segments on Millie. One day when I called her, she was so professional and kept right on asking questions for the article on our visit to Iowa—never letting on people were filming her at the time. The news segment showed her on the phone, and on her large computer monitor were parts of the article that would be published soon after.

By the time of my visit to Iowa, following Millie's footsteps around locations from her childhood in Ladora and college days at the University of Iowa, I was inspired to write her biography. I knew getting the story right would involve intensive research. A lot of surface-level research exists and basic facts have been published for years, with a few more in-depth efforts, such as Melanie Rehak's *Girl Sleuth: Nancy Drew and the Women Who Created Her*. For someone as hard-nosed as Millie, who appreciated honesty and integrity in journalism and writing, I knew I needed to really dig deep to truly do her justice. She wasn't a very open person when it came to her personal life, so discovering just who Millie was and unraveling her journey over the years has been a challenge, but one I've met with determination!

And then there's the whole "angle" issue. "You've got to have an angle on this horsey thing," she'd probably say, something she often said to interviewers. She never knew, though, that I was going to embark on her journey, for she passed away on May 28, 2002, shortly after our Iowa convention. News blanketed the country, and some inaccurate things have been printed, due to misinformation about Nancy Drew's history, but Millie's legacy will always be Nancy Drew, and she knew that before she passed. But her legacy is so much more than Nancy Drew, and I resolved then and there to tell that story too.

In July 2002, the *Toledo Blade* invited me to a private memorial for Millie at the Toledo Club, and that fall our NDS group put on a Millie Benson day at the Toledo-Lucas County Public Library to celebrate her life and all the books and series she'd written. Our local member had collected each of the one hundred and thirty-five books Millie had written, and he set up a display at the library. Today, his collection now resides in The Blade Rare Book Room at the library.

Over the years since Millie passed away, I've written about her and Nancy Drew, among other topics of interest, given presentations about her—including our most recent set of three historic Nancy Drew mini cons that took place in 2015 during all the anniversaries. That year commemorated Nancy Drew's eighty-fifth anniversary and the one hundred and tenth anniversary of Millie's birth and the formation of the Stratemeyer Syndicate. At our second mini con in Toledo during May 2015, NDS sponsored, along with the *Toledo Blade* and The Toledo-Lucas County Public Library, a literary landmark unveiled at the library to honor Millie along with a town council resolution and mayor's proclamation.

THE MILLIE BIO

Since 2002, I have been able to play sleuth—a little bit like Nancy Drew—which I relish. Unraveling the adventuresome tales of Millie Benson has been a most fascinating experience. I have made numerous research trips to Iowa City, Iowa, Toledo, Ohio, and New York City, where the massive Stratemeyer Syndicate files reside at the New York Public Library. I've combined research trips with conventions and other events and, when I could, have fit in research between projects and NDS events—the group has kept me quite busy, as has the consulting and licensing. I've conducted numerous interviews with family, friends, and coworkers. And, most importantly, I've been granted sole access to her personal archive of papers, the first time anyone has been allowed to review the material, so that I can write a truthful, honest, spirited, and, most importantly, definitive biography of Millie.

In 2016, I'm finally categorizing over ten years of research material, including volumes of files featuring original documents once owned by Millie that will eventually find a home in her archive at the University of Iowa. It wouldn't be a story about Millie if it weren't a very intriguing tale—she lived an amazing life, and I've unearthed so many things that no one has a clue about—*yet!* For instance, in the biography you'll learn the true story about her kidnapping in Guatemala and how she used her wits to escape—not unlike infamous sleuth Nancy Drew—how she really felt about Nancy Drew and all the fuss, and we'll dig into mysteries as far back as her college days and her beginnings with the Stratemeyer Syndicate that have yet to be revealed. Her adventures in Central America and her flying escapades around the country will get special focus, as will her favorite series, Penny Parker. We'll also delve into the mystery surrounding her missing autobiography and the map someone drew for me to find it. It was never found, or was it? *Stay tuned . . .* I'm currently writing the biography, *Mildred Wirt Benson—The Real Nancy Drew.*

Visit nancydrewsleuth.com/mildredwirtbenson for more information about Millie and the books and series she wrote.

PHYLLIS KLEIN

Ode to Mildred Wirt Benson
        First of twenty-eight to write Nancy Drew books
            under the Carolyn Keene pen name

So many characters to write
about in a 96-year life. Ghost
writer, snail in a shell.
Can you believe you created
one hundred thirty-five books
of heroines and girl-role models?

And on top of that
you were a jungle traveler,
canoer, air pilot.
All this and also Nancy Drew,
your achievement, girls' rescue
from loneliness, inspiration,
spunky friend,
Nancy, with a flashlight,
intrepid, empowered.
Nancy on a staircase
with another mystery under foot.

Mildred, it took being 95
for you to get a special
Edgar Award from
the Mystery Writers
of America, when you could
finally be the butterfly you always
were. Free of the chrysalis,
Nancy's rightful mother at last,
your blockbuster daughter
bringing you out into the family.

LUISA KAY REYES

Nancy Drew . . .

Since Mildred Wirt Benson could write
Some plots full of daring and might
The syndicate thought
She was just what they sought
To bring their new series to light!

Miss Mildred made Nancy quite bold
But still from the feminine fold
Her brave little sleuth
Could outwit the uncouth
And the Drew girl's adventures soon sold!

With logic Miss Drew hunts for clues
In clocks and in attics or shoes
The criminal set
Know they now have to fret
As Nancy, they just can't confuse!

A local collegian named Ned
On several adventures is led
By Nancy who dares
To explore the thief's lairs
So none of the perps get ahead!

Though many a decade has passed
Since Mildred's first story was cast
The adage holds true
That regardless who's who
With Nancy we all have a blast!

LEA SHANGRAW FOX

Pigeons on your head

"I'll wire the International Federation of American Homing Pigeon
Fanciers and give them the number stamped on the bird's leg wing."

NANCY DREW, *Password to Larkspur Lane*

NOTES FROM THE CONTRIBUTORS

KIMMY ALAN ("Dear Nancy Drew"): I'm not the only boy who read Nancy Drew that ended up having a crush on the teenage redheaded detective. But who could blame us for falling in love with such a positive role model at a time when women were often marginalized in popular literature. Indeed, Nancy inspired women, but she also served as the ideal for what some boys desired in a girl. Adventurous, fun, and intelligent, Nancy was the perfect girlfriend. I chose to declare my love for Nancy Drew books with a personal letter to her. Written with an internal rhyme style I tried to convey my feelings with a bit of flair and rhythm. If any of you should happen to meet her, tell her I'm open to collaboration.

E. KRISTIN ANDERSON ("an attractive girl"): My piece is a found poem from *The Secret of the Old Clock* (New York: Grosset & Dunlap, 1987).

AMANDA ARKEBAUER (Nancy Drew Quilt): My stepmom, Suzi Arkebauer, and I made the quilt in 2001 before there was Nancy Drew fabric. I appliquéd each quilt block (and cross-stitched the Nancy Drew silhouette in the center block) by hand and my stepmom put them together and quilted it for me (with a magnifying glass stitch design in the border). The quilt blocks represent Old Clock, Sky Phantom, Scarlet Slippers, Velvet Mask, Twisted Candles, Broken Locket, Brass-bound Trunk, and Spider Sapphire.

STEVE BOGDANIEC ("Captions Drew Chapter Titles Nancy"): My found poem uses all the captions found with the illustrations in four Nancy Drew books, left in their entirety but presented in a different order. The captions are the first lines of every stanza. The remaining lines are made by mixing the words—minus most of the articles—from the chapter titles of the four books: *The Secret of the Shadow Ranch* (New York: Grosset & Dunlap, 1993), *The Mystery of the Missing Map* (New York: Grosset & Dunlap, 1997), *The Clue in the Old Album* (New York: Grosset & Dunlap, 1977), and *The Mystery of the 99 Steps* (New York: Grosset & Dunlap, 1977).

KATHY BURKETT ("Escape"): "Escape" was created from *The Secret of Shadow Ranch* (New York: Grosset & Dunlap, 1993, 1965, 1931), page 69.

SYLVIA CAVANAUGH ("Mildred Wirt"): My poem uses only letters in the name "Mildred Wirt," the ghostwriter from Iowa who wrote the first three Nancy Drew books.

KRISTINA ENGLAND ("Most of Nancy Drew lives in my garage..."): What can I say about this piece, but that there are many things that conjure up memories of my grandmother these days. She's been gone a little over a year, but had a major influence on my life, even my reading tastes.

JENNIFER FINSTROM ("Nancy Drew's Guide to Life" and "Moxie and Melancholy"): I don't remember a time when I wasn't fascinated by Nancy Drew, and I think my first favorite book was number five, *The Secret of Shadow Ranch*, because there was a horse on the cover. However, my most interesting anecdote involving Nancy Drew is a more recent one. While visiting the annual yard sale in my neighborhood, the first house I stopped at had a cardboard box of an almost complete set of the familiar yellow-covered books. I didn't make it any farther down the block than that house and had to carry the heavy box back to my apartment—but it is to date one of the best additions to my personal library that I've made!

DEIRDRE FLINT ("The Ballad of River Heights"): Many, many of my songs are about childhood and adolescence. I have a song about missing the 70s (Sun In, latch hook rugs, lawn darts), a song about having nuns as teachers . . . Since I spend a whole lot of time up there poking around in the mental attic of my childhood, it's inevitable that I would write a song about Nancy Drew. There was nothing more delicious than the addiction to Nancy Drew because there were *so many* of them. You finish one, and don't have to wait until the author writes another. There's *always* another . . . I sure wish I could find an adult writer that prolific!

LEA SHANGRAW FOX (illustrations on pages 146, 154, 184, and 190): A few years ago I made these digital collages featuring Nancy Drew, mostly inspired by the song "The Ballad of River Heights" by Deirdre Flint (included in this book, starting on page 129). *The Bungalow Mystery* inspired the illustration on page 146, especially the villain Stumpy Dowd. The illustration on page 154 ("You've Been Poisoned") isn't based on any particular story, but was inspired by various Nancy misadventures (getting poisoned, knocked unconscious, bound and gagged). *The Password to Larkspur Lane* and the carrier pigeons that play a role in the plot inspired the illustration on page 184 ("Pigeons on your head"). *The Clue of the Whistling Bagpipes* inspired the collage on page 190.

SHIVAPRIYA GANAPATHY ("Tanka"): I have used three Nancy Drew titles as a beginning for my poem, weaving a tanka around each title.

ERICA GERALD MASON ("mystery and madness"): My piece is a found poem using the titles of the original Nancy Drew books.

KATHLEEN M. HEIDEMAN (illustrations on pages 20, 44, 118, and 140): "Nancy made a wild scramble to save herself" is based on an original drawing by Russell H. Tandy from *The Mystery at the Moss-Covered Mansion* (New York: Grosset & Dunlap, 1941); "I Can't imagine what became of her" is based on an original drawing by Russell H. Tandy from *The Secret of the Old Clock* (New York: Grosset & Dunlap, 1930); "Nancy pulled—Ned struggled—the quicksand" is based on an original drawing by Russell H. Tandy from *The Ghost of Blackwood Hall* (New York: Grosset & Dunlap, 1948).

KATHLEEN HOGAN ("Saving Ned Nickerson"): Nancy Drew was one of my first heroes. She took charge, faced danger, cared deeply about others. I wanted to be like her when I grew up. I am so glad that Silver Birch Press is publishing an anthology inspired by her adventures.

JULEIGH HOWARD-HOBSON ("Unwrapping the 11th Nancy Drew Book at My Birthday Party, 1972"): I found this anthology idea compelling, inspirational, and lovely. I grew up reading Nancy Drew, wishing I was anywhere but in Brooklyn, New York, where there was only crime being solved, not mysteries.

MARK HUDSON (illustrations on pages 74 and 164): I was particularly inspired by the Nancy Drew call to submit something in art, because I believe that many children's books in the past often had good stories, and really good illustrations to encourage a child's imagination. As a child, my parents had me read the Hardy Boys books, and one of the things I liked the most were the illustrations that promised suspense and adventure. I know Nancy Drew was created for young ladies to have a hero, and I feel it's important for young ladies to know they are just as capable of strength and bravery as males. I mostly wanted to capture the spirit of the 1940s or 1950s in my illustrations, and hope I did that.

MATHIAS JANSSON ("Create Your Own Nancy Drew Mystery Story"): My piece is a do-it-yourself Nancy Drew Mystery title generator. Pick something from each of the five columns to create the title of a Nancy Drew Mystery.

ALICE-CATHERINE JENNINGS ("Nancy in Finland"): The inspiration for my poem came from the Nancy Drew mystery *The Secret of the Old Clock* by Carolyn Keene (New York: Grosset & Dunlap, 1930) and the Finnish national epic *The Kalevala,* compiled by Elias Lönnrot and translated into English by Keith Bosley.

JESSIE KEARY ("Murder-Suicide: Nancy Drew and Me"): My poem is based on the Nancy Drew computer game series by Her Interactive, specifically *Curse of Blackmore Manor.*

LAURIE KOLP ("Trapdoors"): My piece is a found poem from *The Bungalow Mystery* (New York: Grosset & Dunlap, 1930).

LORETTE C. LUZAJIC ("Carson's Angels"): My painting features George, Bess, and Nancy. Playing on *Charlie's Angels* with the name of Nancy's father, and referencing the popularity of female detectives or policewomen in today's TV and cinema, the girls are modern with guns. But the painting is also an homage to what Nancy did best for me growing up, which was to ignite my curiosity in the world and allow me to come to terms with the fact that life is a puzzle that no one has figured out. We put the pieces of the mystery together as we go, using the hand we are dealt. All of the imagery underneath the layers is from Nancy Drew books or illustrations. The phrase "life is a mystery" is from Madonna's "Like a Prayer" song, merging a number of pop culture themes to show how Nancy fits in with all of them.

KAREN MASSEY ("Do You Know They Wore Masks"): Last summer, a friend was unloading some books from her childhood when I happened to take a couple of Nancy Drew books to make erasures from. "Do You Know They Wore Masks" is taken from *The Clue in the Jewel Box*, (New York: Grosset & Dunlap, 1943), page 209.

CATHY MCARTHUR ("Nine Years Old: Nancy Drew"): I was an intense reader of Carolyn Keene's work, and was always enthralled by the titles. One day, as an adult I went to a store where they were displayed and began to copy down all of the titles I remembered.

LYLANNE MUSSELMAN ("Solving Mysteries"): I wrote this poem to a prompt for NaPoWriMo: to write a fan letter; instead of doing something "traditional" like writing to a favorite singer or writer . . . I "wrote" to the character Nancy Drew.

SARAH NICHOLS ("An Encounter"): My found poem is based on *The Sign of the Twisted Candles* (New York: Grosset & Dunlap, 1933).

LEE PARPART ("Nancy drew"): "Nancy drew" isn't exactly a short story. It's closer to a piece of conceptual fiction, supported by elements of nonfiction. As some devoted fans of the series will probably recognize, the references to the Stratemeyer Syndicate and Mildred Wirt's job action in the early 1930s are based in fact.

JESSICA PURDY ("Mystery"): I wrote "Mystery" with end-alliteration. I think Nancy herself would enjoy figuring out the "riddle" of the form.

PATRICK T. REARDON ("The Birth of Nancy Drew"): I took a look at the first chapter of the first Nancy Drew book, *The Secret of the Old Clock* (New York: Grosset & Dunlap, 1930). I used and paraphrased phrases from that first chapter to put in a compact, crystallized form what I take to be the essence of the Nancy Drew stories. I used Nancy quotes as the second voice of the back and forth pattern, again words that seemed to capture her essence.

LUISA KAY REYES ("Nancy Drew . . ."): I'm a second generation Nancy Drew reader, as my mother was a huge fan when she was little and I'm a humongous fan, as well. I don't know how many times I've read the classic versions over and over.

M.A. SCOTT ("An Amazing Revelation"): My found poem uses language from a chapter of *The Clue of the Dancing Puppet* (New York: Grosset & Dunlap, 1962).

SHLOKA SHANKAR ("Interior Monologue"): "Interior Monologue" is a found poem taken from Carolyn Keene quotes at goodreads.com (pages 1 and 2).

HILARY A. SMITH: My piece references the page numbers of the original editions of the Nancy Drew Mysteries cited.

MASSIMO SORANZIO ("Time for Mystery, Nancy Drew!"): My poem consists almost entirely of words and phrases making up the titles of Nancy Drew's adventures. Being a boy, as a child and teenager I actually used to read old Sherlock Holmes stories, or in any case detective stories where I could feel involved in the adventures of a male detective; at the time my elder sister started reading Nancy Drew, my favourite crime books were Perry Mason's cases, written by Earle Stanley Gardner. But I remember looking at my sister's shelf, filled with all her Nancy Drew books, and being curious— finding all those titles rather intriguing. Nancy Drew's adventures were published in Italy by Mondadori as a special series for girls, back in the 1970s, with yellow covers like all crime novels, called "i gialli" in Italy ("the yellow [books]") for that reason. I would actually appease my curiosity as a grownup, being rather disappointed when I found out they were not written by one author, but by a number of ghostwriters using the pseudonym Carolyn Keene.

DOROTHY SWOOPE ("You'll Ruin Your Eyes"): Like so many other contributors, Nancy has been a big part of my life. As a librarian for twenty-five years pre-Google, I loved nothing better than solving the mystery of finding the information that people needed and often thought how Nancy had given me that early training!

A. GARNETT WEISS ("With original mystery"): "With original mystery" extracts words from the list of Nancy Drew mysteries on the page preceding the inside title page of *The Hidden Staircase* (New York: Grosset & Dunlap, 1930, 1995 printing).

MARILYN ZELKE-WINDAU ("Long Overdue"): Nancy Drew books were a mainstay of comfort for me as a young girl. I learned from her that it was okay to be a smart girl, to like puzzles, to try to figure out solutions—sometimes creative solutions—and to stick to a problem until an answer could be found. I cherished that alone time with Nancy, reading in bed, under the dining room table, or in the waterless bathtub with blankets and a pillow, door locked so that no one would interrupt me. Most of the books I checked out from the library. They had old bindings. I didn't know then that there were several people who wrote under the pen name Carolyn Keene. Soon, Nancy's mysteries were coming out more and more quickly. My allowance money was always gone at the bookstore. My birthday and Christmas lists became full of titles. I still have most of these books here at home. They stare at me and implore me to remember and reread them.

LEA SHANGRAW FOX

The Clue of the Whistling Bagpipes

ABOUT THE CONTRIBUTORS

KATHLEEN AGUERO's latest book is *After That* (Tiger Bark Books). Her other poetry collections include *Investigations: The Mystery of the Girl Sleuth* (Cervena Barva Press), *Daughter Of* (Cedar Hill Books), *The Real Weather* (Hanging Loose), and *Thirsty Day* (Alice James Books). She has also co-edited three volumes of multi-cultural literature for the University of Georgia Press *(A Gift of Tongues, An Ear to the Ground,* and *Daily Fare)* and is consulting poetry editor of *Solstice Literary Magazine.* A teacher in the low-residency MFA program at Pine Manor College and in Changing Lives through Literature, an alternative sentencing program, she also conducts creative writing for caregivers workshops in both private and community settings.

KIMMY ALAN is a wannabe poet from the land of Lake Woebegone. His talents are not just limited to poetry. He's also a licensed mechanical engineer (aka building boiler operator), busy producing hot air to keep folks warm. His profession also requires him to shovel snow, a task he is not good at, and definitely needs someone to show him how to do it better. A devoted bachelor, he's also known for making fantastic cinnamon rolls, which he himself eats way too much of.

E. KRISTIN ANDERSON is the author of seven chapbooks, including *A Guide for the Practical Abductee* (Red Bird Chapbooks, 2014) *Pray, Pray, Pray: Poems I wrote to Prince in the middle of the night* (Porkbelly Press, 2015), *17 Days* (ELJ Publications), *Acoustic Battery Life* (ELJ, 2016), *Fire in the Sky* (Grey Book Press, 2016), and *She Witnesses* (dancing girl press, 2016). Her nonfiction anthology, *Dear Teen Me*, based on the popular website of the same name, was published in October 2012 by Zest Books (distributed by Houghton Mifflin Harcourt), and her next anthology, *Hysteria*: *Writing the Female Body*, is forthcoming from Lucky Bastard Press. She's worked at *The New Yorker* magazine, has a BA in Classics from Connecticut College, and is currently a poetry editor for *Found Poetry Review* and also edits at *Lucky Bastard.* Her poetry has appeared in many magazines worldwide, including *Room, Hotel Amerika, Barrelhouse, Asimov's Science Fiction,* and *Cicada,* and has work forthcoming in *Folio* and *Indianola Review.* She grew up in Maine, lives in Austin, Texas, and blogs at EKristinAnderson.com.

AMANDA ARKEBAUER is a flight attendant and Nancy Drew collector who lives in Seattle, Washington. Her favorite Nancy Drew book is *The Password to Larkspur Lane.* Highlights of her collection include books signed personally for her when meeting Mildred Wirt Benson, books autographed by Harriett Adams, and original artwork of *The Sinister Omen* by Ruth Sanderson.

ROBERTA BEARY is the haibun editor at *Modern Haiku*. Her book *The Unworn Necklace*, a finalist in the Poetry Society of America's annual book awards, is in its fourth printing. Her most recent book is *Deflection*, a collection of prose poems about loss and grief. Award-winning poet and playwright Grace Cavalieri said, "In *Deflection* she extends her reach with some of the most searingly truthful work I've seen this year." Follow her on twitter @shortpoemz, where she tweets her photoku.

SUJOY BHATTACHARYA is a nature poet from India. At present he is busy with a book of poems on the strangeness of human psychology. He worships humanity and adores poetry as a living deity.

JULIE E. BLOEMEKE grew up in Toledo, Ohio. In researching the pen name Carolyn Keene for "Triple Hoax," she was surprised to discover that Mildred Wirt Benson—the writer largely credited for creating Nancy's personality and sense of adventure—was also living in Toledo during the same time. A poet who now lives in Alpharetta, Georgia, her manuscript, *Slide to Unlock*, was recently chosen by Stephen Dunn as a 2016 finalist for the May Swenson Poetry Award. Her work has appeared in various journals and anthologies including *Gulf Coast, Poet Lore, The James Dickey Review, Bridge Eight*, and *The Great Gatsby Anthology,* among others.

STEVE BOGDANIEC is a writer and teacher, currently teaching at Wright College in Chicago. He has had poetry and short fiction published in numerous journals, most recently *Eclectica Magazine, One Sentence Poems,* and *Blood Lotus.*

ANNE BORN is the author of *A Marshmallow on the Bus* (2014), Prayer *Beads on the Train* (2015), and *Waiting on a Platform* (2016). Her work has been published in the *Newtown Literary Journal* and in the "Me, as a Child" and "All About My Name" Series published by *Silver Birch Press*. She is the editor of *These Winter Months: The Late Orphan Project Anthology* (2016), and her essay on Hillary Clinton's religious faith was included in *Love Her, Love Her Not: The Hillary Paradox*, edited by Joanne Bamberger. Her poetry has been featured in New York at Boundless Tales, Word Up Community Bookstore, and the Queens Council on the Arts. She has been a featured performer with Inspired Word New York City, the New York Transit Museum, and on Queens Public TV in *The World of Arts*. She divides her time between New York and Michigan, and the Camino de Santiago in Spain. Follow her at The Backpack Press and on Twitter, Redbubble, Wattpad, and Instagram @nilesite. Listen to *Born in the Bronx* podcasts on Our Salon Radio.

TANYA BRYAN is a Canadian writer with work published in *Feathertale Review* and the anthologies *My Cruel Invention, Dear Robot: An*

Anthology of Epistolary Science Fiction, and *The Great Gatsby Anthology*. She loves to travel, writing and drawing her experiences, which are often surreal and wonderful. She can be found on Twitter @tanyabryan.

KATHY BURKETT lives in Florida with her husband. She is a high school dropout who eventually earned a BA in English/creative writing. She has been published in various small press publications, including several Silver Birch Press Anthologies, Blood Pudding Press, *Red Fez*, and others. She also makes collage art and odd audio pieces, enjoys cloud watching and playing the kazoo.

BILL CAPOSSERE'S work has appeared in *Harper's Magazine, Colorado Review, Alaska Quarterly Review, Rosebud*, and other journals, as well as in the anthologies *In Short, Short Takes, Man in the Moon*, and most recently *Brief Encounters*. His nonfiction has been recognized in the "Notable Essays" section of several *Best American Essays*, and he has received Pushcart Prize nominations for fiction and nonfiction. His full-length plays *Galileo's* and *Drowned* have both won the GEVA Theatre Regional Writer Showcase contest in recent years and have been given staged readings as part of the Showcase and again as part of GEVA's New Plays Festival. Shorter plays have been chosen for performance by the Rochester Fringe Festival and Rochester's Writers and Books Ten-Minute Play Contests. Other writing includes reviews for the *Los Angeles Review of Books* and regular blogging for Tor.com. He lives in Rochester, New York, where he works as an adjunct English instructor at several local colleges. His education background includes an MFA from the Mt. Rainier Writing Workshop.

SYLVIA CAVANAUGH, originally from Pennsylvania, has an MS in Urban Planning from the University of Wisconsin. She teaches high school African and Asian cultural studies and advises break-dancers and poets. She and her students are involved in the Sheboygan chapter of 100,000 Poets for Change. A Pushcart Prize nominee, her poems have appeared in *An Arial Anthology, Gyroscope Review, The Journal of Creative Geography, Midwest Prairie Review, Seems, Stoneboat Literary Journal, Verse-Wisconsin*, and elsewhere. She is a contributing editor for *Verse-Virtual: An Online Community Journal of Poetry.*

TRICIA MARCELLA CIMERA is an obsessed reader and lover of words. Look for her work (some forthcoming) in these diverse places and elsewhere: the *Buddhist Poetry Review, Dead Snakes, Foliate Oak, Fox Adoption Magazine, Hedgerow: A Journal of Small Poems, I Am Not a Silent Poet, Mad Swirl, Silver Birch Press, Yellow Chair Review* and *Your One Phone Call*. Her poem "The Swear Poem" was recently selected to be in the *Chicago Poetry Press/Journal of Modern Poetry's* Poetry of Protest edition (JOMP 19). Tricia volunteers locally, believes there's no place like her own backyard, and has traveled the world (including Graceland). She resides with her husband and family of animals in Illinois/in a town called St. Charles/by a river named Fox. Nancy Drew is her fave Girl Sleuth but she also has a soft spot for Trixie Belden.

ELLEN COHEN was always the last one up reading a Nancy Drew until well after midnight. Her favorite book is *The Witch Tree Symbol*– probably because it mentions apple schnitzing and shoofly pie. Currently, she is a physician and on the faculty of Harvard Medical School. Still a fan, she keeps her books upright with *Nancy Drew* bookends, and believes the best chapters always end with a cliffhanger.

CHRISTINE COLLIER is a writer from upstate New York, the mother of three, and grandmother to nine. She writes for children's magazines, and is the author of many cozy mysteries, including a four-book series, *The Writer's Club,* and several children's books. Her anthology work has been published by Guideposts, Adams Media, HCI Ultimate Books, Silver Boomer Books, Patchwork Path, Write Integrity Press, and Dancing with Bears.

LINDA CROSFIELD, a resident of Castlegar, B.C., Canada, participates in a month-long postcard poem exchange every August. One year she came across a set of cards depicting the first thirty covers of the Nancy Drew books. This set off such a wave of nostalgia that all month she wrote poems that spoke to the images. She has been published in several chapbooks, anthologies, and literary magazines, including *The Minnesota Review, Labour,* and *The Antigonish Review.*

ASHINI J. DESAI balances creative writing with family, community, and technology management career. Her poems have been published in the anthology *Cities* (2014), a three-dimensional anthology *Overplay /Underdone* (2013), as well as journals such as *Philadelphia Poets* (2009), *Thema* (2007), Asian-American poetry *Word Masala* (2010), and *Yellow as Tumeric, Fragrant as Cloves* (2009). In addition, her essay was included in the anthology *Labor Pains and Birth Stories* (2009). She has written poetry and book reviews for South Asian-centric websites. Her personal website highlighting selected poems is ashinipoetry.blogspot.com.

KRISTINA ENGLAND resides in Worcester, Massachusetts. Her fiction, nonfiction, and poetry have been published in several magazines, including *Apocrypha and Abstractions, Gargoyle, Pure Slush,* and *Silver Birch Press.*

PAUL FERICANO is a poet, satirist, social activist, and co-founder of the parody news syndicate *Yossarian Universal News Service* (1980). His work has appeared in numerous publications since 1970, including *The Wormwood Review, New York Quarterly, The Realist, Charlie*

Hebdo (Paris), *Punch* (London), and *Krokodil* (Moscow). He is the author of several books of poetry, including his latest *The Hollywood Catechism* (Silver Birch Press, 2015). Since 2003, he's directed *SafeNet,* a nonprofit advocacy group that promotes healing for clergy abuse survivors, and writes a column on these issues, "A Room With A Pew (roomwithapew.com).

JENNIFER FINSTROM teaches in the First-Year Writing Program, tutors in writing, and facilitates writing groups at DePaul University. She is the poetry editor of *Eclectica Magazine,* and recent publications include *Autumn Sky, Poetry Daily, Escape Into Life, Gingerbread House Literary Magazine,* and *NEAT.* For Silver Birch Press, she has work appearing in *The Great Gatsby Anthology,* the *Alice in Wonderland Anthology,* and in *Ides: A Collection of Poetry Chapbooks.*

JENNIFER FISHER is a Nancy Drew consultant and author. Her book *Clues for Real Life: The Classic Wit & Wisdom of Nancy Drew* was published in 2007, and she is currently writing a biography of Mildred Wirt Benson, *Mildred Wirt Benson—The Real Nancy Drew.* She is President of the Nancy Drew fan group, The Nancy Drew Sleuths, and plans its annual conventions and handles the officially licensed Nancy Drew merchandising lines. Learn all about Nancy Drew at her website nancydrewsleuth.com and about the Nancy Drew Sleuths fan group and conventions at ndsleuths.com.

DEIRDRE FLINT makes up one forth of The Four Bitchin' Babes, an all-woman band that tours the US. Her music has been featured on TLC and *Nip/Tuck.* She has released two solo CDs, and her other songs include "The Boob Fairy," and "The Bridesmaid Dress Song." She has made great chums during Nancy Drew conventions. Learn more at Deirdreflint.com and Fourbitchinbabes.com.

LEA SHANGRAW FOX has been collecting Nancy Drew books since the age of eight and particularly enjoys the foreign editions of the stories that are published worldwide. She is a member of the Nancy Drew Sleuths fan club and is a regular contributor to the organization's fanzine *The Sleuth.* She maintains the *Around the World with Nancy Drew* website at nancydrewworld.com.

LINDA MCCAULEY FREEMAN has an MFA in Writing and Literature from Bennington College. She is a freelance journalist and columnist for *Living & Being* Magazine and former poet-in-residence of the Putnam Arts Council. Her works have been published in literary journals and anthologized in *Girls: An Anthology.* She has won multiple first-place awards for short stories, and is working on a novel. She and her husband are professional swing dance instructors in the Hudson Valley, New York. Visit her at got2lindy.com.

SHIVAPRIYA GANAPATHY lives in Chennai, India. She graduated with a Masters degree in English Literature, and is now a research scholar working on lesbian feminism and language. She mostly writes in free verse but also dabbles with haiku, tanka, and other Japanese short forms of poetry. Her poems have appeared in *Whispers, Verse Wrights, Word Couch, Wordweavers, Spilt Ink Poetry, Sonic Boom, The Squire: 1,000 Paper Cranes Anthology*, and *The Great Gatsby Anthology* by Silver Birch Press. She also maintains a personal blog and finds writing with a mug of coffee beside her therapeutic.

ERICA GERALD MASON is the author of the poetry collection *i am a telescope: science love poems*. She is a freelance writer and traveling poet. *i am a telescope* is available on Kindle and paperback on Amazon. Find her blog and poetry at ericageraldmason.com.

VIJAYA GOWRISANKAR released her second book of poems, *Reflect*, in December 2015. Her first book, *Inspire*, published in December 2014, reached bestseller status. She was announced as one of the winners of the Inspire by Gandhi competition, organized by Sampad, a U.K. organization, and as the Winner of AZsacra International Poetry Award (December 2015). Her work has been published in *Forwardian, Triadae Magazine, iWrite India, Taj Mahal Review*, as well as *Silver Birch Press*.

GEOSI GYASI is a book blogger, poet, and interviewer. His work has appeared or is forthcoming in *Galway Review, Grey Sparrow Journal, Indiana Voice Journal, Silver Birch Press*, and *Juked*. He is the author of the forthcoming book *Geosi Interviews Fifty Writers Worldwide* (2016) from Lamar University Literary Press in Texas (U.S.). The winner of the 2015 Ake/Air France Prize for Prose, he blogs at geosireads.wordpress.com.

MAUREEN HADZICK-SPISAK is a retired teacher of Reading and English. Her poems have appeared in several anthologies, including *Whispers and Shouts, Paws, Claws, Wings and Things*. The winner of several awards for her poetry, she is part of the Performance Poets Association and reads her poems in bookstores and libraries. She credits her love of reading and writing to Nancy Drew Mysteries.

JENNIFER HERNANDEZ teaches and writes in the Minneapolis area. Her work has appeared recently in *Mothers Always Write, Rose Red Review, Silver Birch Press*, and anthologized in *Bird Float, Tree Song* (Silverton Books). She has performed her poetry at a nonprofit garage, a bike shop filled with taxidermy, and in the kitchen for her children, who are probably her toughest audience.

KATHLEEN M. HEIDEMAN is a writer, artist, and environmental activist working in Michigan's wild Upper Peninsula. Heideman has completed a dozen artist residencies with watersheds, scientific research stations, private foundations, the National Park Service, and the National Science Foundation's Antarctic Artists & Writers Program. She's a curious woman.

KATHLEEN HOGAN is a long-time resident of New York City. She received her BFA from the University of Connecticut.

JULEIGH HOWARD-HOBSON'S poetry has appeared in *The Lyric, Able Muse, HipMama, VerseWisconsin, The Alabama Literary Review, Caduceus, The Liberal Media Made Me Do It* (Lummox Press), *The Best of Barefoot Muse* (Barefoot Muse), *Poem, Revised: 54 Poems, Revisions, Discussions* (Marion Street Press), and other places. Her work has been nominated for both The Best of the Net and The Pushcart Prize. She still loves Nancy Drew, and lives in a small town beside a dark forest, where mysteries of one sort or another often abound, to her great delight.

MARK HUDSON is a poet and writer, artist and photographer whose poetry has appeared on-line in many *Silver Birch Press* series. His work has been most often anthologized in Grey Wolfe publications, and his science fiction poems appear in *Handshake*, an Irregular Science Fiction Newsletter in England.

MATHIAS JANSSON is a Swedish art critic and poet. He has contributed with visual poetry to magazines, including *Lex-ICON, Anatematiskpress, Quarter After #4,* and *Maintenant 8: A Journal of Contemporary Dada.* He has also published a chapbook at *this is visual poetry* and contributed with erasure poetry to anthologies from Silver Birch Press.

ALICE-CATHERINE JENNINGS holds an MFA in Writing from Spalding University. She is the author of *Katherine of Aragon: A Collection of Poems* (Finishing Line Press, 2016), and her poetry has been published worldwide in various literary journals. She divides her time between Oaxaca, Mexico, and Texas, where she lives with her husband, photographer and historian John Mark Jennings.

JESSIE KEARY is a writer and performer living in Chicago. She recently completed The Severn Darden Graduate Program at The Second City Training Center, and is currently working on a collection of prose poetry loosely inspired by *The X-Files.* Follow her on Twitter and Instagram @jessiekeary.

ELIZABETH KERPER lives in Chicago and recently graduated from DePaul University with a BA in English literature. Her work has appeared in *Midwestern Gothic, NEAT,* and *Eclectica,* and she is an associate editor at *No Assholes Literary Magazine.*

PHYLLIS KLEIN believes in poetry. Her work has appeared in the *Pharos of Alpha Omega Medical Society Journal, Qarrtsiluni* online literary magazine, *Silver Birch Press, New Verse News, Crosswinds*

Poetry Journal, and others, and is forthcoming in *Chiron Review*. She is very interested in the conversation between poets and readers of poetry. She sees artistic dialogue as an intimate relationship-building process that fosters healing on many levels. She lives and works in the San Francisco Bay Area as a psychotherapist and poetry therapist. You can learn more at phyllisklein.com.

TRICIA KNOLL is an Oregon poet whose work appears in many journals and anthologies. Her chapbook *Urban Wild* focuses on human interactions with wildlife in urban habitat. *Ocean's Laughter* (2016) combines lyric and eco-poetry to look at change over time in a small Oregon North Coast town. Her website is triciaknoll.com.

LAURIE KOLP, author of *Upon the Blue Couch* (Winter Goose Publishing) and *Hello, It's Your Mother* (Finishing Line Press), serves as president of Texas Gulf Coast Writers and treasurer of the local chapter of the Poetry Society of Texas. Her poems have appeared in *Gargoyle, After the Pause, Crack the Spine, Scissors & Spackle, Pirene's Fountain,* and more. She lives in Southeast Texas with her husband, three children, and two dogs. Learn more at lauriekolp.com.

JENNIFER LAGIER has published ten poetry books and in literary magazines. She taught with California Poets in the Schools and is now a retired college librarian/instructor, member of the Italian American Writers Association, co-edits the *Homestead Review*, and helps coordinate monthly Monterey Bay Poetry Consortium Second Sunday readings. Her website is jlagier.net.

KATHLEEN A. LAWRENCE is an emerging poet who especially likes the challenge of the abecedarian. She grew up in Upstate New York and is from Rochester, the home of the Garbage Plate, Kodachrome, and Cab Calloway. She has been an educator for thirty years, remaining in Central New York in the shadow of the seven hills as a communications professor at SUNY Cortland. Five of her abecedarians recently appeared in the HIV Here & Now poem-a-day countdown.

JENNA LE, Minnesota-born, Vietnamese-American, has a BA in mathematics and an MD. She is the author of *Six Rivers* (NYQ Books, 2011) and *A History of the Cetacean American Diaspora* (Anchor & Plume Press, 2016). Her poetry, fiction, essays, criticism, and translations appear or are forthcoming in *AGNI Online, Bellevue Literary Review, The Best of the Raintown Review, The Los Angeles Review, Massachusetts Review, The Village Voice,* and elsewhere.

JOAN LEOTTA has been playing with words since childhood. She recently completed a month as Tupelo Press's 30/30 poet. Her work has appeared or is forthcoming in *Gnarled Oak, Red Wolf, A Quiet Courage, Eastern Iowa Review, Hobart Literary Review, Silver Birch Press,* and *Postcard Poems and Prose.* She performs folklore and one-woman shows on historic figures, and lives in Calabash, North Carolina, where she walks the beach with husband Joe. A collector of shells, pressed pennies, and memories, she still re-reads Nancy Drew Mysteries. Her second picture book, *Summer in a Bowl,* will be published in fall 2016. Her website is joanleotta.wordpress.com.

KRISTIE BETTS LETTER spent her youth reading Nancy Drew and being suspicious of everyone's motives. Her poems and short stories have appeared in *The Massachusetts Review, The North Dakota Quarterly, Washington Square Passages North, Pangolin Papers,* and *The Southern Humanities Review* (among others). Her novel *Snow and White* was just picked up by KT Literary. She's won several teaching awards for forcing *Hamlet* on high school seniors, and also plays a mean game of pub trivia. Visit her at kristiebettsletter.com or on Twitter @kristieletter.

LORETTE C. LUZAJIC is an artist and writer from Toronto, Canada, where she studied for a bachelor of arts in journalism from Ryerson University. She is the editor of *The Ekphrastic Review: writing and art on art and writing* ekphrastic.net, and the author of over fifteen books of poetry, fiction, and essays on art and culture. She has been published in hundreds of journals and blogs, including *Rattle, Adbusters, Modern Poetry, Grain, the Fiddlehead, Book Slut, Everyday Fiction, the Wonder Café, White Wall Review,* and more. Her short story was recently nominated for Best of the Net. She also incorporates literary themes, poetry, and text into her visual mixed media artwork, which has been exhibited and collected around the world. Visit her at mixedupmedia.ca.

MARIETA MAGLAS has been published in *Ardus, Sybaritic, Tanka Journal, The Aquillrelle Wall of Poetry, A Divine Madness, Near Kin, Poeticdiversity,* and *I Am not a Silent Poet.* She lives in Romania.

KSENYA MAKAROVA lives in a small town in Russia and studies linguistics at a university. She often finds herself drawing fan art of her favorite animated shows and games as NancyKsu, a name inspired by the world-famous female sleuth.

SHAHÉ MANKERIAN's manuscript, *History of Forgetfulness,* has been a finalist at four prestigious competitions: the 2013 Crab Orchard Series in Poetry Open Competition, the Bibby First Book Competition, the Quercus Review Press (Fall Poetry Book Award), and the 2014 White Pine Press Poetry Prize. His poems have appeared in *Mizna.*

SUSAN MARTINELLO lives in Gulf Shores, Alabama. Her poems have appeared in *Grandmother Earth, Birmingham Arts Journal, POEM,* the medical journal *CHEST, Connotation Press,* 2nd *& Church,* as well as *Whatever Remembers Us: An Anthology of Alabama Poetry.*

KAREN MASSEY lives in Ottawa, Canada, near the historic Rideau Canal. Her poetry and erasures have been published online and in anthologies and print publications in Canada, the US, and UK, including the *Bukowski Erasure Poetry Anthology* and *Alice in Wonderland Anthology* from Silver Birch Press, *ottawater, Experiment-O, subTerrain,* and *Inky Needles.* She has two chapbooks from *above/ground press;* the most recent is *Strange Fits of Beauty & Light.*

CATHY MCARTHUR'S (aka Cathy Palermo's) poetry recently appeared in *The Whale Road Review, Pilgrimage,* and *Juked.* She has also published work in *Blueline, Two Hawks Quarterly, Barrow Street, The Bellevue Literary Review,* and in the *Silver Birch Press* "Me as a Child" Series. She lives in Queens, New York, with her husband, and teaches creative writing and composition at The City College of New York.

NANCY MCCABE is the author of *From Little Houses to Little Women: Revisiting a Literary Childhood,* in which she writes about returning to favorite books from her childhood, including the Nancy Drew series. She has published three other books of creative nonfiction and a novel, *Following Disasters* (October 2016). Her work has received a Pushcart Prize and made notable lists six times in Houghton Mifflin Best American anthologies. She directs the writing program at the University of Pittsburgh at Bradford and teaches in the low-residency MFA in creative writing program at Spalding University.

CATFISH MCDARIS won the Thelonius Monk Award in 2015. His words have appeared hither and over yonder. He loves coffee and cats.

PATRICIA MCGOLDRICK is a Kitchener, Ontario, Canada, poet and writer, inspired by the everyday. She is a member of The Ontario Poetry Society and the League of Canadian Poets. Recent publications include the poems "Limerick on Laundry" and "haiku on home" in *Verse Afire* print issues; online titles are posted at commuterlit.com, and in *Red Wolf Journal* you'll find her poem "Urban Upcycling." Visit her at patriciamcgoldrickdocom.wordpress.com or on Twitter @pmgoldrick27.

MICHELLE MCMILLAN-HOLIFIELD studied poetry at Delta State University in the Mississippi Delta. Her work has been included in or is forthcoming in *Boxcar Poetry Review, First Class Lit, The Found Poetry Review, poemmemoirstory, A Quiet Courage, Red Savina Review, Vine Leaves,* and *Windhover,* among others. She is an MFA Candidate at the University of Arkansas/Monticello.

CAROLINA MORALES is the author of four chapbooks of poetry— *Attack of the Fifty Foot Woman* (2015), *Dear Monster* (2012), *In Nancy Drew's Shadow* (2010), and *Bride of Frankenstein and other poems* (2008)—each published by Finishing Line Press. Individual poems have appeared in the *Journal of New Jersey Poets, Nimrod, Paterson Literary Review, Poet Lore, Spoon River Poetry Review,* and other journals. She is a past recipient of scholarships from summer programs at the Fine Arts Work Center in Provincetown, Massachusetts, and the Artist/Teacher Institute at Rutgers-Camden, New Jersey. Her one-act plays have been produced/staged in California, New Jersey, and Pennsylvania.

LYLANNE MUSSELMAN is an award-winning poet, playwright, and artist. Her work has appeared in *Pank, Flying Island, The Tipton Poetry Journal, Poetry Breakfast, So it Goes,* and *Issue 3,* among others, as well as in many anthologies. In addition, she has twice been a Pushcart Nominee. The author of three chapbooks, with a fourth forthcoming, *Weathering Under the Cat,* from Finishing Line Press, she also co-authored *Company of Women: New and Selected Poems* (Chatter House Press, 2013). Presently, she teaches writing at Indiana University—Purdue University Indianapolis (IUPUI) and online for Ivy Tech Community College.

KAITLYNN NICHOL is currently enrolled at Woodbury University, where she is studying for her BFA in Animation and Design. Nancy Drew has been a big part of her life since she was little, from the novels to the games. You can find her either reading or drawing while maintaining a sense of balance in the heat of finals and stress.

SARAH NICHOLS is a writer living in Connecticut. She is the author of *Edie (Whispering): Poems From Grey Gardens* (dancing girl press, 2015), and *The Country of No* (Finishing Line Press, 2012). Nominated for a Pushcart Prize in 2015, her poetry has also appeared in *Yellow Chair Review, The Fem, Thank You For Swallowing, Found Poetry Review,* and the *Noir Erasure Poetry Anthology* (Silver Birch Press, 2013).

FAYE PANTAZOPOULOS is a Greek-American author and poet originally from Lowell, Massachusetts. She lives in coastal Rhode Island with her husband and two Siamese cats. Currently, she is working on a poetry compilation about the muse, and completing a Greek cookbook consisting of family recipes.

LEE PARPART is a media studies researcher who returned to her first passions, poetry and fiction, in 2015. Her essays on Canadian, US, and Irish cinema have appeared in books and journals, and her poetry has been featured in numerous Silver Birch Press series. She won an emerging writer prize in Open Book: Toronto's 2016 "What's Your Story" competition for the Toronto community of East York. Her short story, "Piano-Player's Reach," about neighbors caught up in tensions over a renovation project, will be published on openbooktoronto.ca. She lives in Toronto with her husband and daughter.

STEPHANIE R. PEARMAIN received an MFA in Creative Writing for Children and Young Adults from Hollins University and a BA in Religious Studies and History from the University of Arizona. She teaches courses in Children's & Young Adult Literature and publishing at the University of Arizona and does freelance editing as well. She has been a reader for the Andrea Brown Literary Agency, a reviewer for Children's Literature Database (picture books through novels), and is currently a fiction reader for the online literary magazine *YARN.* Her children's book, *Animal BFFs,* was published by Scholastic in 2012, and a personal essay was published in an anthology by Spruce Mountain Press the same year.

JAMES PENHA is a native New Yorker who has lived for the past quarter-century in Indonesia. He has been nominated for Pushcart Prizes in fiction and in poetry. *Snakes and Angels,* a collection of his adaptations of classic Indonesian folk tales, won the 2009 Cervena Barva Press fiction chapbook contest; *No Bones to Carry,* a volume of his poetry, earned the 2007 New Sins Press Editors' Choice Award. Penha edits *TheNewVerse.News,* an online journal of current-events poetry. Find him on Twitter @JamesPenha.

DAVID PERLMUTTER is a freelance writer based in Winnipeg, Manitoba, Canada. The holder of an MA degree from the Universities of Manitoba and Winnipeg, and a lifelong animation fan, he has published short fiction in a variety of genres for various magazines and anthologies, as well as essays on his favorite topics for similar publishers. He is the author of *America Toons In: A History of Television Animation* (McFarland and Co.), *The Singular Adventures of Jefferson Ball* (Chupa Cabra House), *The Pups* (Booklocker.com), *Certain Private Conversations and Other Stories* (Aurora Publishing), *Orthicon: or, the History of a Bad Idea* (Linkville Press, forthcoming), and *Nothing About Us Without Us: The Adventures of the Cartoon Republican Army* (Dreaming Big Productions, forthcoming).

ROBERT PERRET is a librarian living with his family on the Palouse in northern Idaho. A devout Sherlockian who has published several tales of the Great Detective, he also has a soft spot for girl detectives, mouse detectives, robot detectives—anyone who can deduce, basically. Find out more at robertperret.com.

ANNA PESNELL is a college freshman who began reading Nancy Drew Mystery Stories in second grade. She has since collected the books and PC games and has two special shelves of honor for them and a few other favorite mystery books. She runs a small ND blog and loves making friends who love Nancy as much as she does.

JESSICA PURDY teaches Poetry Workshops at Southern New Hampshire University. She holds an MFA in Creative Writing from Emerson

College. In 2014 *Flycatcher* nominated her for Best New Poets and Best of the Net. She was a featured reader at the Abroad Writers' Conference in Dublin, Ireland, 2015. Recently, her poems have appeared in *Local Nomad, Bluestem Magazine, The Telephone Game, The Tower Journal, The Café Review, Off the Coast, The Foundling Review*, and *Flycatcher*. Previously, her poems have appeared in *Literary Mama, Halfway Down the Stairs, What is Home*, (the 2007 Portsmouth Poet Laureate program's publication), *Analecta*, and *The Beacon Street Review*. In 2015, Finishing Line Press published her chapbook, *Learning the Names*.

CYNTHIA TODD QUAM received an MFA in poetry from Bennington College. She is the author of the chapbook *The Letter Q*, and her work has appeared in a number of publications and literary journals, including *After Hours, Columbia Poetry Review, The Chicago Tribune*, and, most recently, *The Humanist* magazine and TheHumanist.com. She is a freelance writer/editor residing in the Chicago area.

PATRICK T. REARDON, the author of seven books, is writing a history of Chicago's elevated railroad loop and its impact on the development of the city.

NANCY REDDY is the author of *Double Jinx* (Milkweed Editions, 2015), a 2014 winner of the National Poetry Series. Her poems have recently appeared or are forthcoming in *Horsethief, The Iowa Review, Tupelo Quarterly*, and elsewhere. The recipient of a grant from the Sustainable Arts Foundation and a Walter E. Dakin Fellowship from the Sewanee Writers' Conference, she teaches writing at Stockton University in southern New Jersey. Find her online at nancyreddy.com.

LUISA KAY REYES has had poems featured in *I Spy Poetry, A Kaleidoscope of Poetry,* and the *How Sweet It Is* anthologies published by the Stark County District Library. She has also had poems published in *The Sleuth* magazine for Nancy Drew enthusiasts and *The Silkworm* poetry anthology published by the Florence Poet's Society. Recently her poem "A Christmas Poem" was declared one of the winners of the Sixteenth Annual Stark County District Library Poetry Contest. In 2007, she received Honorable Mention in the Alabama Meter Readers International Limerick Contest and First Place in the Florence Poet's Society Limerick Contest.

JEANNIE E. ROBERTS writes, draws and paints, and often photographs her natural surroundings. Her fourth book, *Romp and Ceremony*, a full-length poetry collection, is forthcoming from Finishing Line Press. She is the author of *Beyond Bulrush*, a full-length poetry collection (Lit Fest Press, 2015), *Nature of it All*, a poetry chapbook (Finishing Line Press, 2013), and the author and illustrator of *Let's*

Make Faces!, a children's book (2009). An award-winning poet, her poems appear in online magazines, print journals, and anthologies. Born in Minneapolis, Minnesota, she lives in Wisconsin's Chippewa Valley area. Learn more about her at jrcreative.biz.

STEPHEN D. ROGERS is the author of *Three-Minute Mysteries* and more than nine hundred shorter works. For list of new and upcoming titles as well as other timely information, visit stephendrogers.com.

M.A. SCOTT is a classical musician, collage artist, and writer, currently working as a paralegal. She is a writing student at the Hudson Valley Writers Center, and is coming to poetry later in life as a second creative path.

SHLOKA SHANKAR is a freelance writer from Bangalore, India. She loves experimenting with Japanese short forms of poetry, as well as found/remixed poetry. She also enjoys singing and creating abstract art. Her work has most recently appeared in *Failed Haiku, Otata, Otoliths, Thank You For Swallowing, Right Hand Pointing*, and elsewhere. The founding editor of the literary & arts journal *Sonic Boom*, follow her on Twitter @shloks89.

SHEIKHA A. is from Pakistan and United Arab Emirates. She is the author of a short poetry collection *Spaced* (Hammer and Anvil Books, 2013), available on Kindle. Her work appears in over sixty literary venues, and she hopes to continue getting published widely. In addition, her poetry has been recited at two separate poetry events held in Greece. The poetry editor for *eFiction India*, her published work can be accessed at sheikha82.wordpress.com.

SOGOL SHIRAZI is a pianist and researcher originally from Los Angeles who studied at the Royal College of Music, London, and the Longy School of Music in Cambridge, Massachusetts. She has fond memories of reading Nancy Drew books in her elementary school's library. She lives in Philadelphia, where her work focuses on researching the effect of trauma on the brain.

DONNA JT SMITH's poem "Two Rainbows and the Moon" was published online by *Shadow Express*, and a number of her poems have appeared in various *Silver Birch Press* series. Recently retired from a teaching career, Donna writes and paints on the coast of Maine with her husband, along with a yellow lab and a white cat. The cat, Noah, enjoys helping out with typing. Find her poetry at mainlywrite.blogspot.com.

HILARY A. SMITH is a high school English teacher, avid reader, equestrian, runner, and college football fan. She lives in beautiful Sonoma County wine country.

MASSIMO SORANZIO writes on the northern Adriatic coast of Italy, about twenty miles from Trieste. He teaches English as a foreign language and English literature in a high school, and has been a journalist, a translator, and a freelance lecturer on Modernist literature and literary translation. He took part in the *Found Poetry Review*'s National Poetry Month challenges Oulipost (2014) and PoMoSco (2015), and in a virtual tour around the world with an international group of poets on foundpoetryfrontiers.org.

ELIZABETH STARK is a freelance illustrator and lifelong Nancy Drew fanatic. Her work has appeared in the video game *Nancy Drew: Secrets Can Kill* (2010). When not drawing, she enjoys reading, travel, and photography.

VIRGINIA CHASE SUTTON'S third book of poetry, *Of a Transient Nature*, was published in 2016 by Knut House Press. Her second book, *What Brings You to Del Amo*, won the Samuel French Morse Poetry Prize and was published by the University of New England Press. Her first book, *Embellishments*, was published by Chatoyant. Her poems have won the Louis Untermeyer Scholarship in Poetry at Bread Loaf Writer's Conference and the Allen Ginsberg Poetry Award, and they have appeared in *The Paris Review, Quarterly West*, and *Western Humanities Review*, among other magazines, journals, and anthologies. She lives in Tempe, Arizona, with her husband.

DOROTHY SWOOPE is an award-winning poet whose work has been published in newspapers, anthologies, and literary magazines in Australia, the US, and Canada. She emigrated from the US and now resides on the South Coast of New South Wales, Australia. Her childhood memoir *Wait 'til Your Father Gets Home!* was released in August 2016.

SHREHYA TANEJA has completed her Bachelor's and Master's degrees in English Literature, and is currently pursuing an M.Phil in English Literature, all from Delhi University, India. During the course of her education, she won prizes for her stories and for translation of poems. That's when she decided to try her hand at poetry. She has worked for several online magazines, including *The Indian Fusion, Sambar Vada,* and *The Vibrant Echoes*. Recently, five of her poems have been published in the online magazine *Five* (2016), and her work has also appeared in the inaugural issue of *Opus Journal* (2016), with more to follow. She enjoys observing the different facets of life and talking about them through her work—attempting to weave stories through a few words. Read more of her writing at unpublishedplatform.weebly.com.

MARJORIE TESSER's poems and stories have appeared recently in anthologies and journals, including *Earth's Daughters, Drunken Boat,* and *The Saturday Evening Post*. She is author of poetry chapbooks *The Important Thing Is* (Firewheel Award Winner) and *The Magic Feather* (Finishing Line Press), co-edited the anthologies *Bowery Women* and

Estamos Aqui (Bowery Books) and *Travelin' Mama* (forthcoming from Demeter Press), and is editor-in-chief of *Mom Egg Review*.

MARION TICKNER writes from her home in Syracuse, New York. She has worked with children in the church setting for many years, so it's only natural that she would enjoy writing for them. She has been published in several children's magazines, both print and online. Her stories also appear in several anthologies: *Mistletoe Madness,* edited by Miriam Hees, and *Summer Shorts,* edited by Madeline Smoot (both Blooming Tree Press); *When God Steps In,* edited by Bonnie Bruno; *The Christmas Stocking* and *Treasure Box* (Patchwork Path); books edited by Marie McGaha (Dancing With Bear Publishing): *One Red Rose, Gingersnaps,* and *Candy Canes,* and *Blizzard Adventure* (Kindle only); *Nightlight—A Golden Light Anthology* (Chamberton Publishing); and *God Still Meets Needs,* edited by Mark Littleton. When she isn't writing, you'll find her reading, knitting, or crocheting.

MELANIE VILLINES is a writer and editor who lives in Los Angeles. Her most recent novel is *Windy City Sinners* (Sugar Skull Press, 2015).

SARAH BROUSSARD WEAVER lives in Portland, Oregon. Her work has been published in *The Nervous Breakdown, The Establishment, Literary Orphans,* and *Full Grown People,* among other journals. She can be found at sbweaver.com and on Twitter @sarahbweaver.

MERCEDES WEBB-PULLMAN graduated in 2011 from Victoria University Wellington with MA in Creative Writing. Her poems and short stories have appeared online and in print, in *Turbine, 4th Floor, Swamp, Reconfigurations, The Electronic Bridge, Otoliths, Connotations, The Red Room,* and *Kind of a Hurricane Press.* She lives on the Kapiti Coast, New Zealand.

A. GARNETT WEISS is a Canadian poet whose words appear in local and national media, various chapbooks, literary journals and anthologies, as well as online, either under the pseudonym A. Garnett Weiss or as JC Sulzenko. *Silver Birch Press* has featured her poems in a number of online series, as well as in its *Self-Portrait* and *Ides* anthologies. Her poems also have been published in *Vallum: Contemporary Poetry* and on *Arc Poetry Magazine*'s shortlist for Poem of the Year (2014.) She sits on the selection board for *Bywords.ca* and serves as curator for *The Glebe Report*'s "Poetry Quarter."

LIN WHITEHOUSE lives in a small English village. She works for a children's charity and writes at every opportunity. Her writing has appeared in *Turbulence, Writing Magazine,* and *The Great Gatsby Anthology,* as well as in short story anthologies, including *Whitby Abbey, Pure Inspiration,* and *The Finger.* Her short plays have been performed around East and North Yorkshire and recently as part of 2015 Cornucopia Festival.

LISA WILEY teaches creative writing, poetry, and composition at Erie Community College in Buffalo, New York. She is the author of two chapbooks—*My Daughter Wears Her Evil Eye to School* (The Writer's Den, 2015) and *Chamber Music* (Finishing Line Press, 2013). Her poetry has appeared in *The Healing Muse, Mom Egg Review, Rockhurst Review, Silver Birch Press, Third Wednesday,* and *Yale Journal for Humanities,* among others. She serves as a judge for Poetry Out Loud.

MARTIN WILLITTS JR is a retired librarian. He has been in many of the *Silver Birch Press* on-line series and was featured in the *Alice in Wonderland Anthology.* His poems have appeared in *Blue Fifth Review, Rattle, Kentucky Review, Comstock Review, Centrifugal Eye, Big City Lit, Stone Canoe,* and many others. He has won many national and international individual poem contests, including the *2014 International Dylan Thomas Poetry Award.* He has over twenty chapbooks, plus eleven full-length collections, including the National Ecological Award winning *Searching for What You Cannot See* (Hiraeth Press, 2013), *Before Anything, There Was Mystery* (Flutter Press, 2014), *Irises, the Lightning Conductor for Van Gogh's Illness* (Aldrich Press, 2014), *God Is Not Amused with What You Are Doing in Her Name* (Aldrich Press, 2015), and *How to Be Silent* (FutureCycle Press, 2016).

MARILYN ZELKE-WINDAU is a Wisconsin poet and a former elementary school art teacher. She enjoys painting with words. Her poems and articles have appeared in many printed and online venues, including *Verse Wisconsin, Stoneboat, Your Daily Poem, Midwest Review,* and several anthologies. Her chapbook *Adventures in Paradise* (Finishing Line Press) and self-illustrated manuscript *Momentary Ordinary* (Pebblebrook Press) were published in 2014. *Owning Shadows* is forthcoming in 2017 from Aldrich Press. She adds her maiden name when she writes to honor her father, who was also a writer.

ACKNOWLEDGMENTS

"Larkspur Lane" by Kathleen Aguero was previously published in *After That* (Tiger Bark Press, 2013) and, in a slightly different form, in the chapbook *Investigations: The Mystery of the Girl Sleuth* (Barva Press, 2008).

"valentine's day" by Roberta Beary first appeared in the online journal *Failed Haiku: A Journal of English Senryu*

"It's Not the Books, It's the Library" by Anne Born was previously published in *Prayer Beads on the Train* (New York: The Backpack Press, 2015).

"Nancy Drew's Guide to Life" by Jennifer Finstrom first appeared in the Silver Birch Press "Me, in Fiction" Series at silverbirchpress.wordpress.com (January 2, 2016).

"Nine Years Old: Nancy Drew" by Cathy McArthur first appeared in the online journal *Unpleasant Event Schedule* (2005).

"Coming of Age with Nancy Drew" by Nancy McCabe appeared in a slightly different version in her book *From Little Houses to Little Women: Rediscovering a Literary Childhood* (University of Missouri Press, 2014).

"In Nancy Drew's shadow" by Carolina Morales first appeared in the chapbook of the same name (Finishing Line Press, 2010).

"What Nancy Drew" by Cynthia Todd Quam appeared in her chapbook *The Letter Q* (Bennington College Alumni Chapbook Series, 2002).

"The Case of the Double Jinx" by Nancy Reddy originally appeared in *Anti-,* was selected for *Best of the Net 2011,* and was published in *Double Jinx* (Milkweed, 2015).

"Nancy Drew..." by Luisa Kay Reyes was previously published in the July/August 2013 issue of *The Sleuth,* a zine published by Jennifer Fisher with The Nancy Drew Sleuths fan club.

"You'll Ruin Your Eyes" by Dorothy Swoope appeared in her book *Wait 'til Your Father Gets Home* (Middle Ridge Press, 2016).

INDEX OF CONTRIBUTORS

62180882R00117

Made in the USA
Charleston, SC
03 October 2016